"Why Did You Really Want Me Here This Summer?

"There are hundreds of terrific nannies in New York. You could have had your pick."

"I like your company. I thought you'd enjoy spending a couple months at the beach."

Her scrutiny intensified. "No ulterior motives?"

"Such as?" he prompted, voice silky smooth, wondering if she was brave enough to voice the challenge in her eyes.

"We haven't even been here two hours and already you've kissed me." The exaggerated rise and fall of her chest betrayed her agitation. She was practically vibrating with tension. "Do you expect me to sleep with you?"

"I'm considering the possibility," he admitted.

* * *

The Nanny Trap is part of the #1 bestselling miniseries from Harlequin Desire, Billionaires and Babies: Powerful men... wrapped around their babies' little fingers.

* * *

If you're on Twitter, tell us what you think of Harlequin Desire! #harlequindesire

Dear Reader,

I have always wanted to write a surrogacy story, so when I was offered the opportunity to do a Billionaires and Babies book I knew exactly what story to tell.

Bella McAndrews is a kindergarten teacher from Iowa with a soft heart and a fascination with wealthy New York businessman Blake Ford. She knows he'll never be hers, but she gave birth to his son and that has created a bond between them. One that Blake intends to fully explore.

Most of the book takes place in the Hamptons, a place I've never been, but which feels familiar thanks to all the television shows set there. One of the best things about books is the opportunity to take an armchair vacation. I really enjoyed soaking up some virtual sun and breathing sea air as I followed Bella and Blake's journey to love. I hope you do, too.

All the best,

Cat Schield

THE
NANNY TRAP

—

CAT SCHIELD

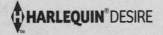

Recycling programs
for this product may
not exist in your area.

ISBN-13: 978-0-373-73266-1

THE NANNY TRAP

Printed in U.S.A.

www.Harlequin.com

One

Sleek black limos were a common sight parked in front of St. Vincent's, one of Manhattan's premier private schools, and Bella McAndrews barely gave this one a thought as she knelt down on the sun-warmed sidewalk to say goodbye to her students. It was the last day of school; a procession of twelve kindergartners hugged her and then ran to waiting vehicles. She bumped her chin against their navy wool blazers, emblazoned with the St. Vincent's crest, her chest tightening as each pair of arms squeezed her. The children were precious and unique and she'd enjoyed having every one in her class. By the time her final student approached, she could barely speak past the lump in her throat.

"This is for you." The boy's blue eyes were solemn as he handed her a pencil drawing. "So you won't forget me."

"As if I could do that." Bella blinked away hot tears and glanced down at the self-portrait. What she held was no ordinary drawing by a six-year-old. Justin had shown talent early and his parents had given him private art lessons. Bella couldn't help but wonder what her brothers and sisters could have accomplished if they'd been given all the opportunities afforded Justin by his wealthy parents.

"This is very nicely done, Justin."

"Thank you." A grin transformed his solemn expression. Before Bella could be glad that he was acting like a normal six-year-old for a change, he became a serious man-child once more. "I hope you have a nice summer," he finished in formal tones.

"You, too."

Pasting on a bright smile, she got to her feet. Inside, her mood reflected the gray sky above. She watched, her chest heavy, until he got into the back of a black Town Car. Most of her fellow teachers were as excited as their students as the end of the school year approached, but Bella wasn't fond of partings. If she'd had her way, she'd keep her kindergartners forever. But that wasn't how life worked. Her job was to guide their growth and prepare them for new challenges. As difficult as it was for her, she had to set them free. How else could they soar?

"Bella."

The sound of her name cut through the excited chatter of children being released from their educational imprisonment. She stiffened, recognizing Blake Ford's deep voice, even though she hadn't heard it since late last summer. A rush of joy rooted her to the spot. Twenty feet away the heavy wood doors of St. Vincent's offered her a place to hide. Common sense urged her to flee. He would be perceptive enough to figure out how miserable she'd been these past nine months and curious enough to wonder why.

Acting as if she hadn't heard Blake, she pivoted toward the school. But before she could escape, she felt Blake's long fingers on her left arm. Apprehension shivered along her nerve endings. The light hold prevented her flight and agitated her pulse. He'd had this effect on her from the start.

Bracing herself against an unwelcome stab of delight, she turned in his direction.

His wide shoulders, encased in gray wool, blocked her view of the street and the long limo parked at the curb. She gathered a deep breath to steady herself and gulped in a heavy dose of Blake. He smelled of soap—the fresh, clean scent of a mountain stream. No fussy cologne for Blake Ford.

Enigmatic. Intense. Brooding. Blake had fascinated and frightened her at their first meeting at the fertility clinic. But the intuitiveness she'd inherited from Grandma Izzy, for whom she was named, had told her to hear him out on that occasion.

She'd come to New York City to be a surrogate for a couple who'd decided to give in vitro a try, but before she could meet with them, the wife's best friend offered to carry their child.

Around the same time, Blake and Victoria had come to accept that a surrogate was the only move left for them. Thinking Bella would be a good fit with the power couple, the doctor at the clinic had arranged for Bella to meet Blake and his wife.

Over a cup of coffee, as Blake and Victoria had shared their deep sadness at their inability to conceive, Bella had decided Blake was more than just the successful, driven CEO of a large investment management firm. He was a man with a deep yearning for family.

"Blake, how nice to see you." Her voice held a breathless edge. She dug her fingernails into her palm and told herself to get a grip. "What brings you to St. Vincent's?"

His hand fell away. He had no need to keep a physical hold on her. His resolute gaze held her transfixed. "You."

"Me?" Her stomach somersaulted. "I don't understand."

They'd not parted on the best of terms. He hadn't understood why she wanted no future contact with his family and she had no intention of enlightening him, no matter how insistently he'd pressed her for an explanation. Where did she start?

Her unexpected and unwished-for reluctance to give up the child she'd carried for nine months? The fact that his wife had told her in no uncertain terms that she was never to contact them again? The way his simplest touch sparked something elemental and forbidden? The certainty that she'd betray her moral code if he gave her the slightest inkling that he wanted her?

"You didn't go back to Iowa like you said you were going to."

She saw an unyielding wall of accusations in his steel-blue eyes. He was annoyed. Not glad to see her. So why had he come?

"St. Vincent's asked me back for a second year." Guilt poked at her, but Bella ignored it. She didn't owe him anything more than the explanation she gave most everyone. The real reason she'd stayed in New York was because she felt connected to the child she'd carried. But the truth was too troubling and deeply personal to share. "They pay better than the public schools back home." During their previous association, she'd let him believe she was preoccupied with money. It had kept him from questioning her motivations. "And I've really grown to love New York."

"So your mother said." He slid his hand into the pocket of his exquisitely tailored suit coat.

"You called my parents?"

"How else did you think I found you?" He regarded her impassively. "She and I had quite a chat. You didn't tell them the truth about what brought you to New York, did you?"

Bella regarded him with exasperation. Should she have shared with her conservative-leaning parents that she'd lent out her womb to strangers for nine months so she could stop the bank from repossessing the farm that had been in her father's family for four generations? Not likely. It was better that they believe she'd taken a high-paying job in New York City and been able to secure a personal loan because of that. Her mother had been very upset with her for going into debt for them, but Bella assured her it was something she felt strongly about doing for her family.

"I didn't want them to worry."

"In the last nine months, I've discovered that worrying is what parents do."

When his attention shifted to the car behind him, she relaxed slightly, happy to have his focus off her. "I imagine you have."

She had worries of her own. Was the child she'd given birth to happy? Did he get to see enough of his busy parents? Were they playing peekaboo with him? Reading him a bedtime story? She hated the ache in her heart. It exposed how badly she'd deceived herself.

"I assume my parents were curious about who you were and why you'd called looking for me. What did you tell them?"

"That I was someone you used to work for."

Which, in a twisted way, wasn't far from the truth. "Just that?" She couldn't believe that her mother had given up her whereabouts to a stranger on the phone. Hadn't she been the tiniest bit suspicious? Of course, Blake had a reassuring way about him. After all, after spending thirty minutes with him, Bella had agreed to act as the surrogate mother to his child. "Or did you have to tell them more?"

"I said you'd taken care of my son and I wanted to see how you were doing."

"I'm doing just fine."

His gaze slid over her as if to reassure himself she was indeed well. "You certainly look great."

"Thanks." While Blake's once-over carried no sexual intent, it still sparked unwelcome heat to run through her veins.

It would be humiliating if he ever discovered how her body reacted to his nearness. "How are you?"

"Busy."

"As usual," she quipped, wringing a disgruntled frown from him. Funny how they'd fallen back into familiar patterns. For a second it was as if three-quarters of a year hadn't separated them. "Always the workaholic."

He shook his head. "Not anymore. You'll be happy to know that I'm home every night by five o'clock. My son is too important for me to neglect."

He spoke firmly, determined to emphasize that his priorities were different from his father's, a man Blake grew up barely knowing because he spent so much time at the office or out of town on business. In the days before Bella had gotten pregnant with Blake and Victoria's baby, she'd been concerned about Blake's long hours, but a serious conversation about his childhood had reassured her that his son would be a top priority in his life.

"I'm glad."

"I know." His granite features softened for the space of a heartbeat, reminding her how he'd looked the day the ultrasound announced he was going to have a son.

Joy caused her pulse to spike. The months apart from him hadn't dimmed her reaction to his every mood. She remained enthralled by his powerful personality and susceptible to the dimples that dented his cheeks in those rare moments when he smiled.

"I knew you'd make a good father." It was why she'd agreed to be the surrogate for his child.

"It's a lot more work than I expected." His eyes lost focus. "And a lot more rewarding."

"How's Andrew?" She'd been equal parts thrilled and dismayed that Blake and Victoria had used part of her surname to christen their son.

"We call him Drew," Blake explained. "He's smart. Curious. Happy."

"He sounds delightful." Her longing to snuggle him—which had dimmed to an ache these past few months—flared up again. Bella crossed her arms against the sudden pain in her chest.

"What are your plans for the summer?"

The abruptness of his question caught her off guard. "My roommate and I are helping her cousin with her catering business." It was something she'd done regularly since moving in with Deidre, except for those months when pregnancy had made it too uncomfortable for Bella to spend hours on her feet. "Why?"

"I need a nanny for Drew this summer. The girl who's been taking care of him fell and broke her leg in three places a week ago and I need someone who can fill in for the next two months until she's recovered."

"Surely there are agencies that can help you out."

"I'm disinclined to look for someone that way. It took me thirty candidates before I found Talia. We are leaving for the Hamptons on Saturday. I'd like you to join us."

Besieged by conflicting emotions, Bella offered a neutral response. "It's nice that you thought of me."

Only it wasn't nice. It was unbearable. Walking away from the child who'd grown beneath her heart had shredded the tender organ. She'd cherished him when he'd been a flutter of movement in her belly. How was she supposed to take care of him for two months and not fall madly in love with his happy smile, his delighted giggle, his sweet scent?

She'd thought being a surrogate would be easy for her. In junior high she'd decided being a mom wasn't for her. She didn't want to be like her mother and have her life revolve around her kids. She'd grown up taking care of her brothers and sisters. She wanted to be free of that sort of responsibility. Being pregnant with Drew had challenged all she thought she believed.

Bella shied away from emotions as dangerous to her soul as splintered glass was to her bare feet. "But I really don't think I can."

He narrowed his eyes at her refusal. "I'll pay you more than you'd make as a waitress."

"That's generous."

Blake believed that she'd only acted as Drew's surrogate because of the money. That was only partially true. As much as she'd needed the money, she'd really wanted to help him and Victoria grow their family. All through her pregnancy, her intention had been to stay in touch. Blake encouraged her to maintain contact with his son, but Victoria had her own ideas.

She'd pleaded with Bella, asking her to stay out of Drew's life so she and Blake could focus on being a family. It was Victoria's right. And no matter how much it hurt her, Bella wouldn't dream of interfering between husband and wife.

"Have you discussed this with Victoria?" His wife didn't want Bella in the same city as Drew, much less the same house.

"She and I divorced two months ago."

"Oh, Blake." The news rocked her. What had happened to Victoria's determination to make her marriage work? It didn't make sense that she'd given up so easily.

"Turns out Vicky didn't take to being a mother." His unhappiness hit her like a January wind and Bella shivered. "She got a supporting role in an off-Broadway play and threw herself into acting."

Regret flared. Victoria had cut Bella out of Drew's life and then left him without a mother. "Did you have any idea she felt this way?"

"No. It came as a complete surprise." Blake's mouth tightened.

To Bella, as well.

Victoria had thrown herself into preparing the nursery and often quoted from parenting books. But it was Blake who'd accompanied Bella to every doctor's appointment while his wife immersed herself in auditions for off-Broadway shows. Bella had been worried about his long hours at the office, even though he genuinely seemed excited to be a father. She'd obviously focused her anxiety on the wrong parent-to-be.

"I'm so sorry."

Impulsively she touched his arm. The contact zinged from her fingers to her heart in a nanosecond, leaving her wobbly with reaction. She pulled back, but too late to save her composure from harm.

If he noticed her awkwardness, he gave no sign. "Now you understand why I need someone I trust to take care of Drew this summer," he said. "I could use your help."

Demands or bribes she could've easily refused. But turning down this request for help was like asking Superman to lift a truck-sized boulder of kryptonite. The superhero couldn't do it. She was no stronger.

And she was handicapped by her memories of her previous visit to the Hamptons. Early-morning walks on the beach. Sipping tea on the wraparound porch. Blake had invited her to spend two weeks at his vacation property toward the end of her pregnancy. The downside had been loneliness and too much time to think, but on the weekends when Blake and Vicky came with friends and family, the enormous house had been filled with laughter and conversation.

"Are you sure you wouldn't be better off keeping him in the city with you?"

"I'm planning on working most of the week from the beach house. I need someone to keep an eye on Drew during the day while I'm occupied. You can have your evenings free."

"How can you be away from the office that much?" Remembering the long hours he'd put in the year before, she couldn't imagine that Drew would get to spend much time with his father.

A ghost of a smile appeared at her shock. "I told you I've changed."

A warm glow filled her as she gazed at him, acknowledging the truth in his eyes. This was the Blake who fascinated her. A man with strong convictions and simmering passions. Intelligent. Wry. Sexy.

Tormented by temptation, she shook her head. A whole summer at the beach? With the son she had no claim to? With the man she had no right to desire?

She was already too susceptible to Blake. What if Drew took up residence in her heart, as well? Forming a lasting attachment to the child she'd carried wasn't part of her plan. After raising her seven brothers and sisters, she'd had enough of being a parent. Freedom was her watchword these days, but being unable to shake her anxiety about Drew's welfare worried her.

"Thank you for the offer. It sounds like a wonderful opportunity, but I have to pass."

A protest gathered on Blake's lips, but before he could voice it, the limo's door opened and an unhappy wail rode the fragrant spring wind blowing straight at them. Blake's tension switched off as his focus shifted to his son.

"Sounds like Drew wants a chance to convince you."

And before Bella could offer an objection, Blake crossed to his driver. The man had fetched the infant out of his car seat and now handed him to Blake. Drew's discontented cries turned to crows of delight as his father lifted him above his head. Bella's mouth went dry at the endearing picture of a powerful businessman in a tailored suit stealing a moment out of his busy schedule to hang out with his adorable nine-month-old baby. The tender connection between father and son made her throat ache.

At last Blake settled the baby against his chest and returned to where Bella stood. "Drew, this is Bella. She's the one I told you about."

As if the child could understand.

But when Drew's blue-gray eyes, so like his father's, settled on her in unblinking steadiness, Bella wondered if she'd misjudged the child's comprehension. She stretched out her hand, hoping that Blake wouldn't notice the slight tremor. Drew latched on with a surprisingly fierce grip. A lump of unhappiness swelled in Bella's chest, making it hard for her to breathe.

"Nice to meet you, Drew," she murmured. And when the infant gave her a broad grin, she tumbled head over heels in love.

While Bella stared at the baby she'd never held, Blake fought to keep his anger from showing. Drew was at his most adorable, plying her with happy smiles, which offered Blake a chance to scrutinize the twenty-eight-year-old woman who'd been his son's surrogate.

Lovely. Like a tranquil lake deep in the forest, her beauty was of the peaceful sort. With her dark brown hair and smooth, pale skin, Bella possessed a Midwestern-girl-next-door look. When he and Vicky had first hired her to act as their surrogate, Blake had worried that a big, impersonal city like New York would chew up an Iowa farm girl like Bella and spit her out. But, raised on love and clear values, she had a steel backbone and a practical view of the world.

Her expression was unreadable as she shook Drew's hand. Didn't she feel anything at all? She'd carried Drew for nine months. Surely that would forge an unbreakable bond. So what had happened? Why, after assuring him that she would be delighted to be a part of their extended family after Drew was born, had she done an abrupt about-face and walked away without a backward glance? Had it all been lies? Had he been so blinded by joy at his impending fatherhood that he'd let her deceive him into believing she was a loving, nurturing person? It wouldn't be the first time a woman had fooled him into seeing her as something she wasn't.

In the days following Drew's birth, he'd fought to keep his disappointment in Bella's startling decision from overshadowing his delight at being a father. The whole time she was pregnant she'd talked as if she would like to stay in touch with Drew. Obviously she'd been lying. Bella had seen acting as a surrogate as a means to fast cash. She'd performed a service. Blake didn't begrudge the money he'd paid her. He and Vicky had been desperate to start a family, and Bella had been instrumental in making that happen. He'd just been so damn stunned that the woman he'd thought he knew had made such a swift and unexpected about-face.

His anger with her for turning her back on Drew was irrational, but it was rooted in childhood hurt. Bella's abrupt departure reminded him how he felt when he was eight and his own mother had abandoned him and his father to return to her old life in Paris. But at least with his mother, and even with Vicky, there had been warning signs that they lacked a maternal instinct. With Bella, he'd been convinced that she was a caring, nurturing woman.

"He's very handsome." She might have been commenting on the weather as she released Drew's hand and stepped back. "He has your eyes."

"And Victoria's iron will." Blake kept his attention fixed on Drew as he reflected on his ex-wife's determination to pursue her career instead of being a mother. No amount of reasoning had convinced Vicky that her place was with her son.

Drew leaned away from Blake's chest, reaching for the ground and babbling insistently. More than anything Drew wanted to be put down so he could explore the unfamiliar place and shove into his mouth whatever he crawled across. He was at that age where it was dangerous to take your eyes off him for a second. Hoping to distract him, Blake pulled out the plastic key ring he'd shoved into his pocket earlier.

Ever since Vicky had walked out on him and Drew, Blake had wondered if Bella would be upset that the child she'd agreed to carry hadn't ended up in a perfect two-parent home. Then again, it wasn't as if they'd sold her a bill of goods. He certainly hadn't suspected that his wife would decide that motherhood didn't suit her less than a month after her son was born.

"You think so?" Bella watched as Drew threw the keys to the ground and renewed his appeals to be put down. "I think determination is a trait he got from his father."

"You make it sound like a bad thing," Blake said. His surly mood wasn't dissipating. Usually the second he hoisted Drew into his arms, all his cares fell away. But seeing Bella had churned up resentment and mistrust. "It's how I keep profits climbing in double digit percentages for Wilcox Investments."

"Of course."

Her dry smile needled Blake. *Damn.* He'd missed her sunny nature and optimism. Her bright mind and Midwestern take on things. While his wife found his business dealings deadly dull, Bella had been happy to listen and quick with questions when she didn't understand something.

He'd thought of her as a younger sister. A friend.

Her abrupt departure from his son's life had been unexpected and unsettling. They'd often discussed what would happen after Drew was born. She'd been excited to stay in touch with Drew, to return to New York City to visit him.

He'd appreciated that she intended to be part of his son's extended family because the closer Bella got to delivering Drew, the more worried Blake had become about Victoria's desire to be a mother. About the time Bella was starting her third trimester, Vicky had gotten a part in an off-Broadway show and started spending less and less time at home, re-awakening the anxiety Blake recalled from the months preceding his mother's move to Paris.

He and Vicky had begun to argue over her priorities. After Drew was born it got worse. She wasn't acting like Drew's mother; rather, she was a stranger who rarely ventured into his nursery. She complained that Blake put too much pressure on her. That his expectations were too much for her to bear. Brief, heated discussions soon led to long, heavy silences. Their marriage was unraveling.

Was it any surprise that she'd ended up having an affair with the show's producer, Gregory Marshall?

Blake's cell phone rang. "Here." He handed Drew to Bella and fished it out of his pocket. While he spoke with his assistant, he watched for some hint of emotion in Bella's face.

She tensed as Drew leaned forward and put his palms on her mouth. They stared deep into each other's eyes while Blake looked on. He wasn't sure if Bella was even breathing. Was she finally feeling something? Getting her to connect with Drew was why he'd approached her about being Drew's nanny. Now that Vicky had walked away from their family, he was damned if he was going to let his son grow up not knowing the woman who'd given him life, too.

"I need to get back to the office," he told Bella, gesturing with the phone toward the limo. "If you wouldn't mind putting him in his car seat."

"Sure."

She headed for the car, moving with a graceful stride that snagged his attention. The pregnancy weight was gone. She was back to the slim, delicate creature she'd been when he'd first met her at the fertility clinic.

She smiled at the driver when he opened the door for her. The car seat was on the opposite side of the vehicle and she had to maneuver to buckle Drew in. She chose to keep one foot on the sidewalk while the top half of her was swallowed up by the limo.

Blake raked his fingers through his hair. She had no idea what a charming picture she presented, her rear end wiggling as she fastened Drew into his safety seat. Abruptly, amusement became something much more compelling. He sucked in a hard breath, besieged by the desire to wrap his fingers around her hips and press up against her delicious curves.

Where the hell had that come from?

"Blake? What do you want me to tell Don?" His assistant's question made Blake realize he had no idea what she was talking about.

"I have to call you back." He hung up on her as the heat surging through his veins showed no signs of abating.

The feeling was as unwelcome as it was unexpected. Not once had he felt the slightest hint of lust toward the young woman while she'd acted as Drew's surrogate. He'd been married, committed to his wife, and it wasn't in his nature to cheat either physically or mentally. Bella had been for all intents and purposes an employee. They'd been friends. Nothing more.

But his marriage vows no longer stood between them and the attraction was an unexpected complication. He strode toward the car, his nerve endings tingling as he drew within touching distance of Bella.

"He's all secure." She backed away from the car, her hands clasped before her. Did she sense the riotous impulses that had surged to life in him, or was she just eager to get away from him and his request?

"Thank you." He gripped the car door, anchoring himself against the compulsion to brush a strand of hair off her cheek. "Having you take care of him this summer will be good for both of us."

"I really don't think it's a good idea, Blake."

Although she had refused his offer, Blake heard less conviction in her voice this time and sensed that Drew had already charmed her into agreeing to join them in the Hamptons.

"It's a wonderful idea. Take the night and think it over." He blasted her with his most engaging smile. "Do you still have my number?"

Lightning flashed in her eyes. The color of much-washed denim. They'd transfixed him from the start.

"Yes," she retorted, her voice gruff.

"Good. If you don't call me by nine tomorrow morning, I'll be forced to track you down again."

"Fine. I'll think about it." It wasn't enthusiastic agreement, but it wasn't a firm refusal either.

"Wonderful."

Despite his need to get going or risk running late for a meeting, Blake's gaze lingered on Bella until she entered St. Vincent's. For the first time since Vicky had abandoned their marriage, he was ready to move his personal life forward. Seeing Bella again reminded him how satisfying his situation had been a year ago. He'd been happily married and anticipating the birth of his son. And then Vicky had left and he was back to feeling incomplete. These past few months he'd known what would make his world whole again. All he needed was the right mother for Drew.

Today, he'd found her.

Two

Still shaken by her encounter with Blake and Drew, Bella let herself into the apartment she shared with Deidre and set a bag of groceries on the kitchen counter. The small two-bedroom was on the Upper West Side of Manhattan, not far from Central Park. Although the unit rented for a little over two thousand a month, because Bella's room was barely big enough for her double bed, her share was only eight hundred. It was a nice deal for her.

The location was a quick walk across Central Park to the school where she and Deidre worked and the low cost enabled her to send money home to her parents and still retain enough for herself. To have some fun. To build a small nest egg. Whatever she wanted.

Financial security was a luxury she'd never known growing up, and the cash cushion she now enjoyed filled her with a sense of power and confidence.

"There you are." Deidre appeared in the doorway to her room, her bright blond curls a wild tangle. She wore workout clothes and her skin had a light sheen of perspiration. "I wondered what happened to you. I'm almost done with my weights routine if you want to head to the park for some cardio."

"A run sounds good." Before stopping at the market to pick up the ingredients for dinner, Bella had taken the long way through the park, hoping the walk would clear her head. The exercise hadn't been strenuous enough. She was no more decisive now than when Blake's limo had pulled away from the curb.

Growing up with a houseful of siblings, the only way she got any peace was to disappear into the cornfields and make her way to the dirt path that led from their farm to the county road. In the winter the snow drifted in the fields, making it harder to escape her seven brothers and sisters, so she usually just sneaked into the barn and hid in the haymow.

"You're awfully quiet," Deidre said, reaching into the refrigerator and pulling out a bottle of water. "Did one of your students go into hysterics because it was the last day of school today and they couldn't bear to be parted from you for a whole summer?"

"What?" Bella shook her head at Deidre's question. "No. Nothing like that."

"I'm surprised. You are everyone's favorite teacher, you know."

"That's sweet, but we had no repeat of last year's drama." Warmed by her roommate's praise, Bella smiled. "I made sure I prepared them better this year."

"So what's up?"

"Blake came by the school today." Although she hadn't told her roommate everything that had transpired regarding the surrogacy, Bella had appreciated Deidre's sensible take on her mixed feelings about giving up Drew.

"Blake?" Deidre's concern reflected in her expression and her voice. "How did that go?"

"A lot better than you would expect, given how angry he was with me last fall."

"What did he want?"

"He wants me to be Drew's nanny for the summer."

Deidre looked appalled. "His nanny? He has a lot of nerve."

Some of Bella's anxiety eased in the face of her friend's fierceness. It was nice to have someone to support her for a change instead of always being the one people leaned on. "He doesn't have any idea how hard it was for me to give up Drew."

The cozy apartment fell away as Bella got lost in the memory of holding Drew. Beneath his soft skin, he was strong like his father. As she'd buckled him into his car seat, she'd inhaled his wonderful baby scent, so like her siblings' when they were little, and yet all his own. It had whipped her emotions into a muddled stew.

As much as she loved helping to raise her brothers and sisters, she'd lost her childhood to changing diapers, calming temper tantrums, making lunches and helping with homework. Her mother couldn't have kept up on her own. Plus there was always something around the farm that demanded Stella McAndrews's attention.

Bella knew she was a lot like her mother. A nurturer. Taking care of people was almost a compulsion. But it had left her little time or energy for herself and in the middle of her sophomore year in high school, she recognized the burning in her gut as resentment. She felt trapped by her siblings' neediness and began questioning her parents' decision to have eight children.

Soon, the farm, the small nearby town where they attended school, even her friends—their dreams no bigger than the rural community they lived in—began to feel like a prison she had to escape.

But to do so, she needed to make plans and promises.

She would focus on doing well in high school so she could get into college. Majoring in education was a logical choice. She'd grown up teaching her siblings and felt a sense of accomplishment when they did well in school.

She loved college and with each step toward graduation her future looked brighter. Between her course load and work, her time was still not her own, but now she was calling the shots and making all the decisions. It was a heady feeling. One she wasn't ready to surrender to a boyfriend. So she didn't date much. If something looked like it was getting serious, she broke it off. She liked her freedom and wasn't willing to give it up.

"He's beautiful." Bella summoned the energy for a weak smile. "Perfect."

"Blake?" Deidre looked puzzled.

Bella shook her head. "Drew."

"You saw him, too?"

"I did more than that." Her throat seized. "I held him."

Deidre made a disgusted noise. "So what was Blake's reaction when you told him no about the nanny job?"

"What do you think?" Bella winced at Deidre's disapproving scowl.

"He badgered you to say yes."

"*Badgered* is a little strong. He just didn't take no for an answer."

"Are you sure you really told him no?"

"I did."

"No hesitations?"

"Of course not."

Bella and Deidre might have started as roommates a year and a half ago, but as the months passed, they'd become good friends. Bella liked living in New York City, but once in a while the distance between her and that crowded farmhouse in Iowa felt farther than a thousand miles. She appreciated having someone to come home to. To cook for and to share the couch with. A friend she could confide in over a bottle of wine. For all her longing to be free, Bella couldn't deny she hated being alone.

"Not even when you picture that gorgeous mansion on the beach?" Deidre persisted.

Bella sighed in appreciation. "You know me too well. Okay, I'll admit the thought of a summer in the Hamptons is very tempting."

Deidre dug Bella's running shoes from under the bed while she changed. "So what are you going to do?"

"I really should turn him down."

"You really should. But are you sure that's what you want to do?"

"I promised Lisa I'd help with her events this summer."

"And you always keep your promises."

Bella thought about her bargain with Blake's ex-wife. Accepting the job as Drew's nanny wouldn't technically be breaking her promise to Victoria because their divorce meant the reason Bella had agreed to stay away no longer existed. Her presence in their life couldn't be considered a distraction to the tight family Victoria had hoped to have with Blake and Drew.

But staying out of Victoria's way hadn't been the only reason she'd cut off all contact. Bella had begun feeling things that ran contrary to what she'd determined for her life, and the conflict had disturbed her.

"I'll call Blake as soon as we're back from our run and tell him I can't be Drew's nanny."

"Why not now?"

"Because I need to plan what to say or he might just talk me into it."

As the limo eased toward the curb in front of his stepsister's building, Blake gathered up the baby and his bright blue diaper bag. Slinging it over his shoulder, lips quirking

as he contemplated how becoming a parent had domesticated him, Blake strode into Jeanne's building, nodding at
the doorman as he passed.

"You're late," his stepsister announced when he stepped
off the elevator. She raised her arms in welcome as she advanced to take her nephew. Murmuring in soothing tones,
she plucked Drew out of Blake's arms and cuddled him.
"I've been worried."

"I had to make a slight detour." Blake smiled when Drew
latched onto Jeanne's chunky gold necklace and blinked
sleepily up at her.

"Well, you're here now and just in time to hear my wonderful news." Jeanne's gaze cut to her stepbrother. "We're
going to be neighbors this summer. Isn't that great? Now
you don't need to worry about a nanny for Drew. I can take
care of him until Talia gets back on her feet."

"You found a rental this close to summer?"

"Connie and Gideon are getting divorced and they can't
agree on who gets the beach house, so they're letting Peter
and me lease it. We'll be living two doors away. It'll be such
great fun. Of course, Peter will only come up on the weekends, but I'm planning on spending as much time as I can
at the beach. Isn't it wonderful?"

"Wonderful," Blake echoed, his voice flat. He hadn't yet
shared his summer plans with Jeanne because he was certain she wouldn't approve. "But you don't need to watch
Drew this summer. I found someone to fill in as his nanny."

"Oh." Jeanne looked disappointed. Two months ago she'd
found out she was having a baby and her maternal instincts
had kicked into high gear. "I was hoping to spend the summer with my nephew. I hope the woman comes from a reputable agency."

"I didn't use an agency." Blake decided to deliver his news
without preamble. "I asked Bella."

"Oh, Blake, no."

He ignored Jeanne's dismay. "You knew that she's been working at St. Vincent's this past year, didn't you?"

Jeanne had been the one who'd gotten Bella a job at the prestigious school a year ago last fall. It was her husband's alma mater and the endowment they gave to the school each year gave them a certain pull when it came to asking favors.

"Yes," his stepsister admitted with an exaggerated sigh.

"Why didn't you tell me?"

"Wasn't it you who said she didn't want to have anything to do with Drew?" Jeanne hadn't liked Bella, but she'd never explained why. "Why would you want to bother with her?"

Because he hadn't been completely satisfied with Bella's explanation for why she wanted to sever all contact. Because for reasons he couldn't rationalize, something unfinished lay between them.

"I need a nanny for Drew for a couple months until Talia's broken leg heals." This was what had prompted him to start looking for Bella. But it turned out that wasn't his only reason for tracking her down.

Jeanne's brow creased. "Let me help you hire someone."

Why couldn't she understand that he didn't want just anyone? "I'm leaving for the Hamptons in two days. I don't have time to interview a bunch of candidates. I know Bella. I trust her with Drew."

"Do you think that's wise?"

"Not only did she help raise her brothers and sisters, but she's a kindergarten teacher. Who could be better?"

"I don't think this is a good plan, Blake." Jeanne carried the sleeping Drew to the portable playpen set up in her stylish living room and settled the baby, fussing with his blanket until she was satisfied. "Bella declined contact with Drew. No pictures or updates. Why do you think she'd want to take care of him for two months?"

Jeanne's skepticism echoed Blake's own concerns. "She'll

do it." The money he intended to offer would be hard for her to refuse.

"Pick someone else. Anyone else."

"Why?"

"That girl is trouble."

Jeanne's proclamation was so ridiculous, Blake laughed. "Bella? She's the furthest thing from trouble."

"Are you going to tell me you never noticed the way she looked at you?"

Blake's amusement dried up. "What are you talking about? She and I were friends. Nothing more."

"Maybe nothing more from your perspective, but I think she was more than half in love with you." Jeanne crossed her arms and frowned. "Not that I blame her. You are wealthy, handsome and charming."

"In that order?" Blake muttered, unsettled by the interest that had flared inside him. Was Bella attracted to him? Maybe that's what accounted for his unexpected awareness of her—he was merely responding to her subliminal signals. Body language. The chemistry of pheromones. Building blocks of sexual desire. Easy to disregard now that he knew the root cause.

"But the two of you together alone in the Hamptons will give her ample opportunity to get her hooks into you."

"That isn't going to happen."

"No?"

"First of all, I believe I have some say in who I get involved with." Blake arched his eyebrows when Jeanne opened her mouth to protest. "Secondly, Bella isn't interested in getting her hooks in me. You said it yourself. She declined any contact with Drew. She told me she doesn't want to be a mother. She did enough parenting with her siblings. So you don't need to worry that I'm going to do something as foolish as fall for her."

"That's good to hear. But hasn't it occurred to you that

Drew needs more than a series of nannies? He needs a mother. Someone who will love him with all her heart."

"I've been thinking along those lines myself."

First Bella had turned her back on Drew. Then Vicky. He could do nothing about the latter. His ex-wife had let him believe she wanted a family when what she really wanted was for their relationship to remain unchanged, but Bella's values were different. She'd come from a large family. And if he'd learned anything at all about her in the months before Drew was born, he'd seen that she had a nurturing nature. Even if she was determined to deny it.

With Vicky there'd been no such mothering instinct. His ex-wife had insisted on hiring a nanny before Drew was born. She maintained she didn't have the temperament to be a full-time mother. He should have listened to her. But he'd been too set on having his son grow up in the perfect family Blake had not had growing up.

Jeanne lit up. "I'm so glad to hear you say that."

"Glad why?"

"Victoria ended her relationship with Gregory." His stepsister's animated expression warned Blake she was in full interference mode.

He'd heard something to that effect. "I suspect that had something to do with the fact that her play closed after two weeks?" Blake made no effort to hide his cynicism.

"That's not it at all," Jeanne insisted. "She never stopped loving you."

"She loves her career more."

It had been a bitter blow when he'd discovered how she'd fooled him into believing having a family was her first priority when her true passion was show business.

"That's not true," Jeanne insisted.

While Blake admired Jeanne's loyalty to her best friend, he was in no mood to forgive his ex-wife. "I know you want to defend her, but you're wasting your breath trying to convince me to take her back. She put her career before her family."

"I know it's something she'd never do again."

Despite her conviction, his stepsister's argument failed to shift Blake's opinion of Vicky's desires. "She left me. She left Drew." And it was the latter that prevented him from trusting her ever again.

"She knows she made a mistake."

"A mistake?" Past and present betrayals tangled in Blake's chest. "She chose her career over our family. That's more than just a mistake."

"You are not an easy man to please, Blake," Jeanne said, her tone firm. A second later, she put her hand on his arm. "She was overwhelmed at suddenly becoming a mother and retreated into something that was comfortable and familiar to her. She knows she didn't make the best choice."

"But she made it." He set aside his past disappointments and turned his gaze once more to the future. "And I made mine." Seeing that they weren't ever going to agree, Blake bent down and kissed his stepsister's cheek. "Drew needs a mother."

"And Vicky is ready to be that."

Blake shook his head. "She's not, and I need to put Drew's needs first."

"What does that mean?"

"I got married the first time because I fell in love, and it left my son without a mother. This time I'm going to do it differently."

Three

When Bella finished tying her shoes, she and Deidre left the apartment. They used the three-block walk along Eighty-Ninth Street to warm up their muscles. Reaching the park, they quickly stretched before starting off on an easy jog north along the bridle path. The two-and-a-half-mile run would be relatively easy, but long enough for Bella to reach that place where her mind opened up.

While their shoes thumped rhythmically on the pavement, Bella pulled crisp, fragrant air into her lungs and glanced around her. Late spring had always been her favorite time of year on the farm. Dreary skies, cold and snow gave way to green pastures and new life. It was time to stop planning and take action. Possibilities seemed as boundless as the fields that surrounded her family's farm.

It was no different in New York. As soon as the first buds formed on the trees, she'd felt a kick of excitement, as if anything she wanted could be hers. She and Deidre had begun to make plans for the summer and tossed ideas around for a winter vacation. And now that school was out, she reveled in her freedom from responsibility. Her life was turning out exactly the way she wanted.

"Do you ever regret it?" Deidre asked as their run wound down.

"Regret what?"

"The whole surrogacy thing." Obviously Bella hadn't been the only one mulling over her situation during the twenty minutes they'd been running. "I know you say you don't want to get married and have kids, but being pregnant and giving up the baby, that's different."

"I knew what I was getting into." She was a farm girl— when she was six she'd learned a difficult but important lesson about the difference between pets and livestock. As much time and energy that she put into raising a prizewinning calf, there was always a chance that it would be sold. "I wouldn't have done it if I thought I would have a problem. Besides, Drew isn't my baby. He belongs to Blake."

"And Victoria," Deidre prompted.

Bella shook her head. "She left him. Left them."

"What?"

"That's why he needs a nanny this summer. Victoria decided she didn't want to be a mother." Of course, she wasn't Drew's biological mother, but only Victoria and Bella knew the truth about that.

"So what are you going to do?"

"I don't know."

"A little sea air might be exactly what you need."

"Maybe." She wasn't thinking about sea air; she was mulling over the weeks of sleepless nights when she'd be battered by temptation, knowing Blake would be dreaming peacefully in the master bedroom down the hall. Keeping her attraction hidden had been easy when he was married to Victoria. That was a line she'd never cross. But now that he was single, would she send out vibes without even knowing it?

How humiliating to be fired from a nanny job because she had the hots for her employer.

Uncomfortable with the direction her thoughts had taken her, Bella made sure to shift the conversation away from Blake and Drew during the walk back to the apartment. Deidre had called dibs on the first shower, so Bella headed to her bedroom to pack away the supplies she'd brought home from her classroom. By the time she finished, she was ready to call Blake and turn down his offer. Picking up the phone, she noticed she'd missed a call during her run. The message was a giddy explosion of good news from her sister Kate: she'd been accepted into a global health program in Kenya.

It was impossible for Bella not to smile at her sister's enthusiasm. Kate had set her sights on this program since she'd started college three years ago and had worked diligently toward the goal. She would graduate next year with a major in social work and intended to get her master's in public health. Bella couldn't be more proud.

Kate was well on her way to making a life for herself beyond the fetters of the farm and her siblings' constant drain on her energy and resources. It was the dream Bella had for all her siblings, but thus far only Kate and Jess were poised to achieve it.

The phone rang before Bella had a chance to dial Kate's number to congratulate her.

"Hiya, Bella." It was Jess. At eighteen, she was the most practical of Bella's three sisters.

"What's up?"

"I heard Kate leaving you a message and just thought you should know that she's probably not going to be able to afford the semester abroad."

Bella's good mood crashed and burned. "Why not? Last I heard she'd gotten the scholarship and had enough saved." Kate had been working so hard for the past three years to make this trip happen.

"There were some extra costs she hadn't accounted for and Mom and Dad weren't able to give her the money she was counting on."

"How did that happen?" The long pause that followed Bella's question told her everything she needed to know. "What broke down?"

"The tractor. It was in the middle of planting. Mom and Dad didn't have a choice."

"Of course not," Bella mumbled bitterly and felt a stab of guilt over her tone.

It didn't do any good to complain that the money to fix the tractor was supposed to be given to Kate to make her dream come true. Their parents sacrificed so much to keep the farm running and raise a family. Clothes wore out before they were replaced. Food was home cooked and simple. Entertainment consisted of the games they played in their living room or around the dining table.

"I know she'd never ask," Jess continued. "But is there any way you can help her out? I'm giving her five hundred." Money earmarked for her college tuition next year. "Mom's going to give Kate the six hundred in egg money she'd put aside for Sean's truck."

Jess's voice trailed off. Guilt wrenched at Bella. What a horrible sister she was to selfishly cling to her nest egg when Kate needed help. This particular program was only offered once a year. She had to go now, because next year she would begin her graduate studies and the window would be closed.

But Bella had already sent money home to help with Paul's community-college expenses and Jess's activities. She'd helped with the medical bills when Scott broke his leg last fall and contributed to Laney's orthodontic treatments. As hard as her parents worked, sometimes they were caught short financially and Bella's sense of responsibility kicked into overdrive. How could she not help out her family when she had the resources to do so? But every once in a while, she wished there wasn't always someone needing something.

"How much is she short?"

"About three thousand."

Bella's heart sank, but she kept her dismay out of her voice. "Let me see what I can do."

"You're the best," Jess crowed, her unselfishness making Bella feel worse and worse about her resentment. "Elephant shoes."

"Elephant shoes right back," Bella echoed, her family's endearment failing to give her mood the lift it usually did. Shoulders slumping beneath the weight of responsibility, Bella dropped the phone onto her bed.

"Oh, dear." Deidre spoke from the doorway. "Which one of them called this time?"

"Kate and Jess. Kate got into the Kenya program, but she doesn't have enough money to go."

"And she wants you to help her out."

"She would never ask."

"But Jess would."

Bella nodded. Why deny it? Deidre knew how much Bella helped out her family. "It's only three thousand."

"That's the money you were going to use for our trip to the Virgin Islands during Christmas vacation."

"How could I possibly go and enjoy it if I didn't help Kate?"

"I get that, but why do you always have to be the one who gives up what you want to do?"

"Because I'm the oldest." Bella sighed. "And because I can."

"Don't beat yourself up for wanting to say no. You are always there when someone needs you. It's okay not to be once in a while."

"I know. It's just…" Bella trailed off, already knowing she wasn't going to disappoint her sister.

Deidre rolled her eyes. "You're just too responsible for your own good."

"If I was really responsible, I'd be living closer to home so I could be there when Laney needed help with math or Ben wanted to practice his goaltending skills." Instead, she'd stayed in New York, because here she could go hours without feeling weighed down by the never-ending demands of her large family.

"You need to stop feeling guilty for enjoying living so far away from Iowa." Deidre pulled the towel from her hair and wrapped it around her neck. Her brown eyes drilled into Bella. "Stop beating yourself up just because you like the freedom you have here. Your parents decided to have eight kids. They're the ones who should worry about taking care of your brothers and sisters."

"Worrying about each other is what families do." But Bella recognized the disparity between what she said and how she felt. She was burdened in equal parts by guilt and resentment.

"But at some point you're going to have your own family to focus on. What happens to them then?"

Bella shook her head. They'd had this conversation multiple times, but Deidre never listened. "I might someday get married, but you know how I feel about having kids. I don't want any."

"Your family really did a number on you," Deidre said, her expression glum. "You had to grow up way too fast."

"It's not their fault." But there was no denying that the yoke of responsibility Bella had shouldered at a young age had led to her decision never to have kids of her own. Just the thought of being trapped the way her mother had been filled her with dread.

It was why she'd thought she could carry a baby for Victoria and Blake without fear of becoming emotionally involved. Too bad she hadn't understood that her fundamental nature hadn't been altered by her frustration with her family's neediness. If she had, she'd have known she'd fall in love with the child she'd given birth to. A child she had no legal claim on.

"You know," Bella began, her pragmatic side taking over, "if I nanny for Blake this summer, I could afford to help out my sister and have enough for our Caribbean trip."

It was a job that would pay well. She needed the money. With it she could go on vacation this winter and feel no guilt, plus she could replenish her nest egg and still help out her family.

"I think it's a huge mistake."

"Seems more like a win-win situation. I get money. Blake gets a nanny."

With her head cocked to one side, Deidre studied her friend. "You forget that I know how hard it was for you to say no to Blake about staying in touch with Drew. And I know why you did it. Now that Blake is divorced, the reason you agreed to stay out of Drew's life no longer exists."

Bella felt a flutter of excitement in the pit of her stomach. Deidre was right. Blake wasn't married to Victoria any longer, so Bella's promise to disappear and give the three of them a chance to become a family was no longer binding.

But her agreement with Victoria wasn't her only reason for staying away. Giving up Drew had been the hardest thing she'd ever done. Being on the fringe of his life would never allow her ache for him to dull.

"Plus," Deidre continued, her eyes narrowing, "there's that little crush you have on Blake."

"Crush?" Bella's voice wobbled when she tried to sound indignant. "I don't have a crush on Blake."

"I think you do. Imagine all those lovely moonlit nights in the Hamptons. Perfect for romantic walks on the beach. A midnight swim, just the two of you. Clothing optional."

Deidre's eyebrows wagged suggestively. "You'd fall hard for the guy before the first week was over."

"Midnight swims? Romantic walks?" Bella gave a disgusted snort. "Not likely. I'll be sacked out. Exhausted from taking care of Drew all day, and Blake will be attending parties. Now that he's single again, he'll be swamped with invitations." Bella could see she wasn't getting through to her friend. "Besides, there's never been any hint of attraction between us."

"Of course not. He was married."

"He was in love with his wife. For all I know, he still is. They haven't even been divorced two months. I'm sure he isn't ready to move on."

"Keep telling yourself that, and when Blake suggests a nightcap one night after you put Drew to bed, call me the next morning so I can say *I told you so.*"

To Bella's dismay, a delicious, forbidden anticipation began to build. Crossing her arms over her chest, she felt the rapid pace of her heart and tried to ignore her body's troubling reaction to Deidre's warning. It was ridiculous to imagine Blake being interested in her. Her own feelings were more difficult to dismiss.

"That won't happen."

"It might if you spend much time around him."

"Any time we spend together will be with Drew for company. Nothing is going to happen between us."

"A baby in the house isn't going to stop a man like Blake Ford from taking what he wants." Deidre raised her eyebrows suggestively.

"That's not Blake's style." As tempting as it was to ponder whether Deidre was onto something, Bella knew better than to indulge in daydreams. "Blake and Drew are a package deal and he knows I'm not interested in having a family. He'll find someone who wants the same things he does."

"I think you're kidding yourself if you believe you'll ever

be happy without children of your own and a man at your side to share the responsibility with you."

Bella shook her head. "I'm sure my mother thought the same thing when she married my dad. But what happens when the responsibility gets to be too much for the two of you to handle?"

"So marry someone wealthy. Then you'd have staff to take care of your every desire, not to mention your kids." Having delivered her final bit of wisdom, Deidre retreated down the hall, leaving Bella to ponder her roommate's advice.

Would she be as reluctant to have children if money wasn't an issue? Bella had no clear answer. On the day she'd turned fifteen and had to spend her birthday in the emergency room because her two youngest siblings had stuck M&M'S up their noses on her watch, she'd decided she never wanted the responsibility of motherhood. Her opinion didn't change through college or the next few years of teaching when she'd moved away from the farm, although she continued to lend her family what support she could by sending money home. But it was never enough.

The emotions stirred up by her pregnancy had called into question a decade of wanting nothing but her freedom. She'd been plagued by doubts. Questioned her choices. But after Drew's birth, she'd decided that she'd been a victim of pregnancy hormones. Her heart continued to hurt at the absence of Drew from her life, but she knew he was part of a loving family that had his best interests at heart.

Only today she'd discovered that he might have a father who loved him dearly, but the woman who was supposed to be his mother had turned her back on him. Disgust rose at Victoria's actions. If Bella had suspected how things would turn out, she never would have agreed to carry Drew for Blake and his wife.

So what was Bella's responsibility to the child now? With Victoria out of the picture, Bella could be a part of Drew's life. Was that what she wanted? To be half in his life, always there, but never truly belonging? Blake had wanted her in his son's life before. But how long would it last? What happened when he remarried? Surely his next wife wouldn't want her around any more than his last one had.

There were no easy answers.

"So you're going to do it." Deidre shook her head as she came back into the room.

"I have to." Bella wished her friend would understand.

"You're going to miss a fabulous summer here. A friend of my brother works the door at that new club everyone has been talking about. He said he can get us in whenever we want."

Disappointment stirred. The reason she'd stayed in New York City was so she could enjoy being young and not have to be responsible for anyone but herself. Last summer she'd been pregnant, so this year she'd been looking forward to dancing the night away at the clubs. Sleeping late. Reading in the park. Being Drew's nanny meant she wouldn't get to do any of that.

But she'd have a week in the Caribbean to look forward to. And she had to help her sister.

"That club sounds like it's going to be so much fun. I wish I could be here to enjoy it with you."

"Then tell Blake to forget it. You don't have to make everyone around you happy all the time."

"I know that."

"But you never put yourself first. Does your family even appreciate all the things you do for them?"

Bella's spine stiffened. "They aren't taking advantage of me." This wasn't the first time Deidre had criticized her for helping her family. Being an only child, she didn't understand why Bella couldn't ignore that her family needed her help. She might feel anxious about working for Blake this summer, but she was willing to do it for Katie. "Look, if I can help my sister and go to the British Virgin Islands later this year, it will be worth spending a couple months as Drew's nanny."

Deidre stepped forward, her expression contrite. "I'm sorry if I made you feel bad. You know what you're doing. Let's go out tonight. You can borrow my new Michelle Mason dress. We'll celebrate the end of the school year and three months of freedom."

"Thanks," Bella said, grateful to have what she'd always wanted.

Freedom to do whatever she wanted with her time. Freedom to live where she was most content. Freedom to spend money on a fabulous vacation without guilt.

So, with all that freedom to revel in, why did she feel as if something was missing?

In the quiet Upper East Side apartment, Blake thanked his doorman and hung up the phone, his spirits lightening. Once he put Drew to bed, his mood always dipped. In the days before his son's arrival, he'd discovered just how much he hated being alone. Most nights Vicky had been at the theater preparing for her off-Broadway debut. The part had been small, but she'd been thrilled. Blake had indulged her, knowing his wife needed a diversion. Waiting to become parents had been hard on both of them.

Or so he'd thought.

It was his nature to be focused and driven. Setting goals and achieving them had made him wildly successful in his business. He'd applied the same principles to his personal life: first finding the perfect woman to marry, and then starting a family with her.

He'd taken Vicky at her word when she told him she wanted children someday. Two months after their divorce was final, he wasn't sure if she'd really wanted to be a mother before being an actress came along and got in the way, or if she'd told him what he wanted to hear so that he'd marry her.

Either way, the results were the same. He and Drew were alone—the same way Blake and his father had been in the ten years following his mother's return to Paris—and Blake had no intention of letting his son grow up without a mother who loved him.

The doorbell chimed, startling Blake out of his reverie. He glanced at his watch as he headed for the front door. Ten-thirty was late for his sister to be out. But when he opened the door, he saw it wasn't Jeanne.

Rocking her weight from one black stiletto sandal to another, Bella looked like a kid caught midprank. But she wasn't a kid. Nor was she the guileless Iowa farm girl she'd been last summer. In the nine months since he'd last seen her, New York City had transformed her into a sophisticated woman who looked at ease in a one-shoulder black mini-dress that showed off miles of toned leg and bared slender arms adorned with eight inches' worth of jangling bracelets.

Her inability to meet his gaze gave him hope that the woman he'd befriended wasn't gone, only hiding beneath her expensive wardrobe. She'd done something with brown eye shadow to make her large, pale blue eyes dominate her face. Not even the bright red she'd applied to her lips could eclipse their haunting beauty. But the stark color did emphasize her mouth's downward cant. The urge to smear her perfect lipstick with hot, demanding kisses demonstrated that his reaction to her this afternoon hadn't been a fluke.

Damn this sudden attraction.

He didn't want to be distracted from his important mission by a fleeting, if forceful, craving to take her to bed. He had to keep the focus on Bella and Drew's relationship. She needed to become so attached to Drew that she couldn't imagine not being a part of his life. That would be jeopardized if Blake got physically involved with her.

He stepped back. The move wasn't an invitation for her to enter, but a retreat from the way she affected him.

"Come in," he offered, covering his lapse of control.

"I can't stay long. I'm meeting friends." She glanced around as she took three steps into the foyer and stopped.

Blake shut the door, trapping them together in the foyer's dimness. Intimacy crowded them as the silence lengthened.

A year ago they'd been friends. He'd thought her one of the kindest, warmest people he'd ever met. She was everything he imagined the perfect mother to be. Gentle, but resolute. A natural caretaker with a loving heart. Dedicated to her family.

His heartbeat quickened as images of her in the apartment rushed through his mind. The evening she came over for dinner to celebrate her agreeing to act as their surrogate. The afternoon she'd perched on the edge of a chair in the living room while they awaited the results of her pregnancy test. Her, cranky and uncomfortable the morning before she gave birth, four days past her due date and annoyed with him for being so positive despite the extended wait.

Thinking about that day made his heart clench. Twenty-four hours later, she'd exited his son's life without a backward glance. "What brings you by?"

"I came to tell you my decision."

"You could have called." He softened his tone to take the edge off the words. A hint of anxiety tightened his muscles. Having her company in the Hamptons this summer was instrumental to his plans. Unfortunately, at the moment he wasn't thinking as a father concerned about his motherless child, but as a man who knew how to appreciate a beautiful woman.

"I should have." She gnawed on her lower lip. "But something has come up and I was wondering if I could borrow three thousand against my salary before we leave New York."

Any elation he might have felt at her decision was tempered by her request. He'd hoped that meeting Drew would have made his offer irresistible, but here she was thinking only of the money. "I think that can be done."

He tightened his jaw against the urge to ask why she needed the money. He'd paid her thirty thousand dollars to act as Drew's surrogate. Had she gone through all that money already? If that was why she'd agreed to be his nanny for a couple months, getting her maternal instinct to kick in might be more of a challenge that it was worth.

"Thank you." She sounded very relieved.

He paused, considering her. "Don't you want to know how much I'm going to pay you?"

"I know you'll be fair."

"Ten thousand."

Her eyes widened. "Very fair."

"Never fear, you'll earn it."

As if to punctuate his statement, a wail came from his study, where Blake had left the baby monitor.

Her gaze reached beyond him, delving into the apartment. "Is Drew still up?"

"No. I put him down an hour ago."

That caught her attention. "You put him down?"

"I am his father."

"Of course you are."

"You didn't expect me to take care of my own son?"

"It's not that."

"Then what?"

A line appeared between her delicately arched eyebrows. "I guess I never pictured you doing anything so domestic."

"You don't think I'm domesticated?"

That made her lips soften and the edges curve up. "Not really."

He wasn't sure what to make of her smile or the way such a minute shifting of facial muscles made his gut twist. "I assure you, I'm quite tame."

"Then things have changed a lot since Drew was born."

"And it's those changes that brought us to where we are right now."

"You mean being a single dad."

"Partially." He noted her quicksilver frown and guessed he'd sparked her curiosity. Before she could question him further, he said, "I'm planning to head to the beach house on Saturday. Can you be ready?"

"Sure. All I need to pack are some shorts and tops."

"And a bathing suit. Drew loves the water."

"Since your current nanny is out of commission, do you want me to stop by tomorrow and help Mrs. Gordon pack for Drew?"

Blake wasn't surprised by her offer. He'd noticed that Bella often went that extra mile when it came to helping people out. "I'm sure she'd appreciate that."

"Tell her I'll be by around ten."

She was turning to go when Blake spoke. "Want to help me check on him?"

The impulsive request caught both of them by surprise.

Bella gestured over her shoulder. "If I'm late my friends will worry."

"I understand." But he didn't move from the foyer, despite his son's continued distress. "Text them. Tell them where you are."

His reluctance to let her go wasn't logical or sensible. Until he'd gone to her school today, he hadn't realized just how much he'd missed her company. The way her eyes danced with mischief. How easily she made him smile.

He'd spent the past nine months being angry with her; it had blocked out all the good memories. Now, thinking back on how well they'd gotten along and confronted with his startling sexual attraction, Blake was forced to face that his plan was not going to be as straightforward as he'd originally thought.

"They're waiting for me." She sidled toward the door, but her attention remained on the source of the unhappy sounds deeper in the apartment. "You'd better go see what's wrong."

And she was out the door before his emotional chaos sorted itself out. He headed to his son's room, contemplating the changes in Bella.

The city had hardened her. Her warmth was no longer as accessible as it once had been. Of course, their final conversation right after Drew's birth hadn't been in any way congenial. He'd been harsh, caught off guard by her insistence that she wanted no contact with Drew.

He still didn't fully believe her explanation. The decision had been such an about-face from everything he believed he knew about her. Well, he would have two uninterrupted months to get to the bottom of her abrupt turnaround.

And before those months were up, he expected to excavate all her secrets.

Four

Little about Blake's East Hampton home had changed since she'd been here last summer. Painted a soothing pearl gray, trimmed in white, it was expansive and elegant on the outside, with dormer windows that overlooked the sprawling front lawn and gardens. Now Bella stood in the middle of the elegant entry drinking in the vast open floor plan before her attention was drawn to the expensive white furniture.

Everything about the house inspired awe. Including the owner.

Blake stood before the two-story windows at the back of the house, staring toward the beach. Bella couldn't see past his broad shoulders, clad in a pale blue oxford button-down, to see the pool and glittering ocean beyond. Behind him, a large portrait of his ex-wife stared at him from above the fireplace.

Casting about, Bella noticed several other photos of the stunningly beautiful Victoria Ford, alone and smiling blissfully from the circle of Blake's arms. Given how dismissive he'd been of his ex-wife and her disregard for her son, she was surprised so many mementos had been permitted to remain.

"I'll have Mrs. Farnes remove those," Blake said, noticing what had captured her interest. "Damn," he muttered. "There's probably more in the master bedroom." Blake crossed the room with his long, hungry stride and plucked Drew from her arms, tossing the infant into the air. The boy's delighted cries drowned out the thump of Bella's heart as she watched father and son. "And while we're at it, we'll have Mrs. Farnes ship the pictures to Victoria in New York."

Tearing her gaze from Blake's relaxed face, Bella strode into the living room and took stock of all the potential trouble the nine-month-old boy could get into if she took her eyes off him for a second. "The house could use some baby proofing."

An unhappy wail followed her words. Bella glanced over her shoulder at the truculent child. Drew wanted to be put down. The forty-five-minute helicopter ride from the East Thirty-Fourth Street heliport hadn't been particularly restful for Bella, but Drew had taken full advantage of the rocking motion and napped. This meant he was full of energy and ready to go.

"Tell Mrs. Farnes what you need done," Blake said, giving in to Drew's demands to be put down.

The baby crawled to the couch and stood up. He required very little help to stay standing. She'd already observed how confidently he walked as long as he had something to hold on to. In no time at all, he'd be walking on his own. Then running. Bella sighed.

"Hello?" a female voice called from the entry. "Anybody home?"

While Blake headed to the front door to greet his stepsister, Drew began working his way along the couch. Bella wished Blake had mentioned that Jeanne would be staying with them this weekend. She would have appreciated the opportunity to prepare herself for the other woman's chilly dislike.

Bella raced forward and caught Drew's hand before it snagged a heavy crystal bowl on the end table.

"Where's my darling nephew?" Jeanne called, sweeping into the living room with great style. She wore a melon-hued linen dress that drew attention to her perfect complexion and played up the reddish highlights in her dark brown hair. A diamond tennis bracelet glittered at her wrist as she descended on her nephew, hands outstretched.

Bella backed away from Drew as his aunt reached him. Jeanne had a knack for making Bella feel like an employee—necessary when the socialite needed something, forgotten otherwise.

"You are going to love it in the Hamptons," she crooned to Drew, snuggling him close despite his incoherent protests. "We are going to have so much fun this summer."

Dismayed to hear that Jeanne would be around so much, Bella glanced in Blake's direction and discovered he was directing the man who'd picked them up at the East Hampton airport on where to put their luggage. The caretaker—Blake had introduced him as Woody—had already brought in several bags belonging to Drew and Blake and had fetched her single suitcase. Alarm stirred as he headed upstairs with it.

"Wait," Bella called after him. "That's mine. It belongs in the pool house."

Blake stopped her. "You'll be staying in the house. I thought it best if you slept across the hall from Drew."

She'd expected Blake would assign her the same accommodations as last summer and was distressed by the idea that she would be sleeping a short distance from him. "Why?" she blurted out.

"He's been waking up in the middle of the night lately. I've been having a hard time getting him back to sleep. I thought you'd have better luck."

"Oh, sure," she said, failing to keep the dismay out of her voice.

"Problem?"

She couldn't help but feel as if the walls were closing in on her. This was how it began with her family, too. She'd agree to a simple request to adjust a hemline and the next thing she knew she was sewing a brand-new dress.

"You did mention that I could have my evenings off."

"Is it your plan to be out all night?" Blake glowered at her.

She steeled herself against a sudden thrill, reminding herself that his concern about her going out—and staying out—was because he expected her to be at Drew's beck and call. Not because he wanted her company himself.

"Of course not." She'd much rather spend her nights with Blake and Drew, but he couldn't know that. He'd start wondering why. "It's just that I was hoping to have a little fun this summer and I really enjoyed the pool house." She'd appreciated the privacy. If not the solitude.

"And I'd like you to be close by."

"Blake, let the girl stay in the pool house if that's what she wants," Jeanne broke in, her exasperation plain. "I really don't see why she's here at all. I'm perfectly capable of watching Drew this summer."

Jeanne's negative attitude toward her had never been this overt and Bella wondered what she'd done to turn the woman against her.

Blake's stepsister gave up the battle with the squirmy Drew and set him down on the foyer's cool marble. Immediately he began crawling toward the open door. Bella chased after him, deciding it would be easier to wear out the adventurous infant than to try to contain him. Glad to escape the stare-down between siblings, Bella scooped up Drew and marched him outside.

"You will be far too busy lunching with friends and shopping to be a full-time babysitter," Blake countered, his voice calm but steely. "Bella will give him her full attention."

To keep him out of trouble, she'd have to. Bella steered Drew away from roses that flanked the sidewalk and aimed for the large expanse of smooth, green lawn. As soon as she'd gauged Drew was a safe distance from the flowerbeds that enclosed the mansion in graceful, bright waves, she plopped onto the grass with a heavy sigh and began tickling Drew's round belly.

His hearty giggles made her smile. She lost herself in his darling grin and ran her fingers through his soft hair. Sighing, she snuggled him close and imprinted his scent in her memories. He endured it all with good humor and took his own turn investigating her nose and mouth with his chubby fingers.

The late-afternoon sunlight cast long shadows across the lawn and Bella knew she couldn't hide out here with Drew much longer. The wind coming off the ocean was growing cooler by the minute. She was psyching herself up to return to the house when she heard the slam of a car door and an engine starting.

Glancing over her shoulder, she spied Jeanne's silver Lexus heading away from the house and Blake striding across the lawn toward them. Her pulse jerked erratically at his somber expression and she wondered if he was going to send her back to the city.

"Where's Jeanne going?" she asked, startled when he sat beside her.

Hoisting Drew onto his lap, Blake stared after his sister. "She's heading home."

"Back to New York?" It distressed Bella to think she'd come between the siblings.

"She and Peter have a rental just down the beach."

"Then she's not staying here?" She couldn't stop relief from overwhelming her voice.

"No." Blake's eyebrow lifted. "I take it you're glad."

Bella plucked at the lawn. "Your sister doesn't like me."

"It's not that she doesn't like you," he explained, weariness twisting his mouth into an unhappy line.

"You could have fooled me."

"She doesn't want us spending the summer together." Blake was watching Drew crawl toward a butterfly that had flitted across his path and spoke almost absently.

"Why not?"

"She thinks you have feelings for me."

Bella couldn't have been more shocked. "What?" she sputtered, sounding anything but amused or incredulous. She sounded guilty. "That's crazy."

Blake's gaze sharpened as it swung in her direction. "I don't know. She was pretty convinced. It was something about the way you looked at me last year."

Sucking in a breath, intending further protest, Bella was silenced by the heat in his eyes. The chilly afternoon suddenly seemed like a midsummer scorcher.

"She's making that up." Bella quivered. "I've never thought of you as anything more than a friend. You were married."

"I'm not married anymore." His fingers grazed her cheek and slipped beneath her hair.

Her nape tingled as he stroked her skin.

"Sure. But that doesn't mean anything has changed."

"Hasn't it?"

Transfixed by the intent glowing in the blue-gray depths of his eyes, she forgot to breathe. The desire that had haunted her for months exploded in her midsection. Reason melted like spring snow on a sunny day.

She wanted him. Badly.

"Tell me you've never imagined me kissing you," Blake demanded, cupping the back of her head and urging her forward. He frowned as the distance between them narrowed.

This could not be happening. If he came any closer, she was going to make a huge fool out of herself.

"I've never."

His lips stopped a mere whisper from hers. "Say it again and make me believe it."

"I've—"

He didn't let her finish.

Blake meant the kiss to put an end to his craving for her. A quick taste and she'd be out of his system.

That's the way it was supposed to work. He didn't expect her soft moan to scatter all rational thought. Or the way her lips parted beneath his to rob him of control. He'd intended to keep the upper hand, but when her fingers tunneled into his hair and tightened almost painfully, he lost the willpower to set her free.

He rubbed his mouth back and forth against hers, felt her body soften. Almost from the first, she surrendered herself completely to the moment. To him. Despite her earlier protests, she offered herself without reservation.

Deepening the pressure on her mouth, he let his tongue slip past her even, white teeth. He thrust into the warm wetness of her mouth, licking at all the sweetness awaiting him. Her ardent reception evoked another moan. This one his.

In a flash he knew this was no experiment. It wasn't going to end easily with him lifting his lips from hers. Stopping the kiss was going to take effort. Way more than it should.

Heat poured through him. He was consumed by desire. Intense. Inappropriate toward the woman who was his son's nanny.

Right and wrong. Simple and complicated.

This had been a mistake. But one he wasn't going to quit making until it was certain to haunt him for the rest of the summer. Maybe beyond.

Drew's sharp cry sliced through the air, severing their

kiss. Bella jerked away and scrambled to her feet faster than Drew could draw breath for a second shriek. Cursing the way his heart was pounding, Blake followed her across the lawn to where his son sat on the grass, his features crumpled in torment.

Recognizing that it wasn't a regular old temper tantrum, Bella had fallen to her knees beside Drew. Her hands skimmed over his face and arms, searching for the damage. Blake joined them just as she found the red spot on the back of his hand.

"I think he was stung by something." She scooped the child into her arms and held him close. "You poor baby."

"Are you sure he was stung?"

Bella shot him a stern look. "I grew up on a farm. I know what a sting looks like." She cupped Drew's cheek and surveyed him. "Is there any history of allergic reactions to bees or wasps in your family?"

"No." He helped her stand, hating the feeling of helplessness that always came over him when Drew cried. "Do you know what to look for if he has a reaction?"

"Difficulty breathing. Severe swelling."

"Someone in your family is allergic?" he quizzed, concern growing as he imagined Drew being afflicted by those symptoms.

She shook her head. "No, but I had a student who carried an EpiPen in case she got stung, which of course she did. About a week into my first year as a teacher. Luckily our classroom was close to the playground so we could get the epinephrine into her before her throat swelled shut."

As they reached the house, they met up with Mrs. Farnes at the front door. She looked from Drew to Bella.

"What's happened?"

"He's been stung," Bella answered, her pace slowing as she entered the house.

"Wasp or bee?" Mrs. Farnes quizzed, catching Drew's

flailing hand so she could peer at the red spot. "Looks like it's swelling some."

"I didn't see a stinger, so I'm assuming it was a wasp." Bella shifted Drew higher on her hip. "Do you think you could pour some vinegar in a bowl?"

"Of course." Mrs. Farnes raced back to the kitchen.

Bella followed, wiping tears from Drew's cheeks as she went.

"Vinegar?" Blake demanded, suspicious.

"It's what we always used on the farm. The acid neutralizes the venom."

"What about a doctor?"

She kissed Drew on the temple and snuggled him close. "He's not showing any signs of a reaction. I think he'll be just fine once his hand stops hurting."

As difficult as it was to entrust his son's welfare to another person, Blake knew that if he interfered, he would disrupt the attachment sparking between Bella and Drew. And this was exactly the sort of situation where Bella shone. Taking care of someone who needed her was as natural as breathing for her. She just needed to stop denying who she was.

Drew's sobs had devolved into ragged inhalations that shook his whole body, followed by a keening cry that had Bella blinking back tears of her own. Blake watched them. Was this the moment Bella transformed into a concerned parent, or was she merely distraught because Drew was so upset?

"All set," Mrs. Farnes said, gesturing to the kitchen table where she'd set a bowl and some dishcloths. "I gave you some ice as well to numb the area. Is that all you need? I could make a baking soda paste."

"My mother never had much luck with baking soda." Bella sat down with Drew in her lap. She dipped a towel in the water and applied it to the back of his hand.

While Drew screamed with renewed enthusiasm, Blake marveled at the range of home remedies these two women knew. He hunkered down beside his son and touched Drew's cheek.

"He seems hot," Blake said.

"I'm not surprised," Mrs. Farnes murmured, handing Drew a cookie. "He's worked himself into quite a lather. This should help."

Hiccupping, Drew stuffed the cookie into his mouth. He smacked noisily, distracted from the pain in his hand. Bella and Mrs. Farnes exchanged a knowing glance. As the level of estrogen in the room peaked, Blake was assailed by a renewed sense of urgency. Drew needed a mother who would tear up when he was hurt and fiercely protect him from the world's dangers. She would teach him respect for women and how to be both strong and gentle at the same time.

He would not grow up with a hole in his heart and a head full of questions about why his mother had abandoned him.

"I think it's working," Bella said, her gaze shifting to Blake. "Will you hold him for me while I fix a bottle?" She dipped the cloth in the vinegar once more and handed it to Blake before she shifted Drew to him. Her fingers slipped over Blake's hand as he sat down, the tender contact a warm reminder of their earlier kiss. "He's going to be all right," she told him softly, her voice encouraging.

Blake tracked her progress across the kitchen, his skin tingling in the aftermath of her light touch. She'd managed his worries over Drew's wasp sting with the same calm reassurance she'd used with his son. As much as she denied that she was cut out for motherhood, she was a natural. More than a natural. She was innately driven to make those around her happy.

The large kitchen became more homey as the smell of cooking onions filled the air, the sound of them sizzling in the pan blending harmoniously with the hum of female voices as Mrs. Farnes began dinner preparations.

Lifting the damp cloth off Drew's wasp sting, Blake noticed the red mark on his son's hand had been reduced to a dot the diameter of a pencil. The progress pleased him.

"It looks a lot better," Bella commented, peering over Blake's shoulder.

Her dark brown hair fell forward, brushing his cheek. He had a quick second to fill his lungs with the scent of vanilla before she swept the wayward strands behind her ear. While she peered at Drew, Blake studied her profile. Her nose had a slight bump from being broken when she was ten while rescuing her three-year-old brother from a charging billy goat owned by her grandmother.

It was the only imperfection in an otherwise lovely face. Softly rounded cheekbones, a well-shaped mouth and pale blue eyes that tilted up at the corners gave her a fresh, girl-next-door look so unlike his ex-wife's sleek sophistication. Combine that with a smile that went from uncertain to delighted in the blink of an eye, and Blake had a hard time keeping his mind focused on his plans and off the delectable kiss they'd just shared.

Already he'd done something he'd intended to avoid. But what Jeanne had said to him about Bella finding him attractive had been gnawing at him. He'd gone over every memory he had of Bella and found no sign that she'd been anything but friendly toward him. Today he'd thrown Jeanne's words in Bella's face, expecting her to hotly deny it. Instead, her protest had lacked conviction. He'd expected her to slap his hand away. To get angry.

His groin stirred at the memory of her impassioned moan. She'd sounded both confounded and thrilled. Beneath his kiss she'd come alive. Her ardent surrender had carried both of them into a place where they alone existed. Blake frowned. How far would things have gone if Drew hadn't brought them back?

"Here's his bottle."

While he'd been lost in thought, Bella had finished preparing Drew's bottle. She held it out to Blake, but he shook his head.

"Why don't you feed him," he said. "I have to call Jeanne and tell her I'm not going to make dinner."

"You shouldn't cancel on your sister," Bella said, carrying baby and bottle out of the kitchen. "Drew is fine. After he finishes this, we're going to read a little and if he isn't sleepy, I'll give him some dinner, a bath and then straight to bed."

Her words had set the scene for the sort of evening he'd been hoping to enjoy, just the three of them.

"You were pretty determined that your nights would be free, remember?" Blake had followed her into the living room. "Besides, I don't feel right about leaving Drew after what happened."

She settled onto the pale blue couch and started feeding Drew before she answered. "Really, Blake, it's only a wasp sting. He's perfectly fine and there's no need for you to stay."

"Are you trying to get rid of me?" He sat beside her, immediately realizing he was too close when his thigh bumped against hers. The contact delighted him. So did the way she bit down on her lower lip.

"Of course not."

"I don't believe you."

She shifted on the soft cushion, but there was nowhere for her to go. He'd boxed her in.

"It has nothing to do with you. I don't want your sister thinking you don't trust me to take care of Drew."

"She'll understand that I'm staying home because otherwise I'll be wondering how he is the whole time and be terrible company."

"She's going to blame me for not keeping a close enough e on him."

"I will tell her it was my fault." Blake's lips thinned. "I'll xplain I had you thoroughly distracted."

"You really shouldn't do that." Concern thrummed in her oice. "She will think we're…"

A rosy flush spilled over her cheeks. The sight of it conounded him. Why was she acting embarrassed? The kiss ney'd shared had given him a clear picture of the attraction etween them. She'd responded boldly to every sweep of his ongue. He hadn't anticipated that she'd throw herself into ne kiss with sweet abandon, or that he'd be equally swept way by the softness of her skin and the heat of her mouth.

"That we're…?" He prompted.

She kept her attention fixed on Drew. "Why did you kiss ne?"

Her voice was so low he almost didn't catch the question.

"Because I wanted to."

"It complicates things between us."

More than she knew.

"Things are already complicated between us."

She eyed Blake as she handed him the empty bottle. "Why id you really want me here this summer? There are hunreds of terrific nannies in New York. You could have had our pick."

"I like your company. I thought you'd enjoy spending a ouple months at the beach."

Her scrutiny intensified. "No ulterior motives?"

"Such as?" he prompted, voice silky smooth, wondering f she was brave enough to voice the challenge in her eyes.

"We haven't even been here two hours and already you've issed me." The exaggerated rise and fall of her chest berayed her agitation. She was practically vibrating with tenion. "Do you expect me to sleep with you?"

"I'm considering the possibility," he admitted. At some

point during that explosive kiss, he'd lost control. Her effect on him was both intriguing and disturbing.

"You don't mean that."

Blake forced his tone neutral. "I do."

"But you've never given any indication that you're interested in me." Her soft blue eyes grew incredibly large in her pale face.

"As you pointed out earlier, I was married. These days I'm free to be attracted to any woman I want."

"Sure, but there are hundreds for you to pick from who are much more suitable."

"Maybe I'm not looking for suitable." He took her chin and forced her to meet his gaze. "Maybe all I'm interested in is a woman who moans when I kiss her."

Her lips parted on a sharp inhale. "You caught me by surprise."

"And if I gave you fair warning? Would that make a difference?"

"You can't be serious."

He stared at her soft mouth, remembering how it felt beneath his. The passionate tangle of her tongue with his. If Drew wasn't snuggled in her arms, his eyes focused on Bella's face, Blake would lean over and show her just how powerful the chemistry between them could be.

"Would you like me to demonstrate just how serious I am?"

"No." She shook her head vehemently. "Don't toy with me, Blake."

"I assure you, that's the last thing I intend to do." Deciding he'd pushed her to the very edge of her comfort zone, Blake got to his feet. "We'll talk more about this later. Right now I need to change if I'm going to make it to Jeanne's on time."

Brain reeling from her exchange with Blake, Bella stared after him. What had she gotten herself into? Had coming to e Hamptons with Blake and Drew been a huge mistake? he last thing she'd ever expected was that Deidre would ave been right about Blake. What had his kiss meant? Was he a naive fool to read anything into it at all?

Blake was single. She was a warm body. Was it as sim-le as that? But why would he choose her when the Hamp-ns were filled with far more suitable women? Maybe she houldn't ask questions. Maybe she should just pack and et the hell out.

Unfortunately, now that she'd given her sister the three-housand-dollar advance on her salary, she would have to tay and be Drew's nanny for at least two weeks.

Besides, she couldn't just leave father and son in the lurch. To matter how often she tried to put her needs first, it was hevitable that she would put acting responsibly before self-reservation. She was trapped here. Incarcerated by her be-ief system.

When Blake came home from his stepsister's dinner party, he would simply tell him that nothing like that kiss could ver happen between them ever again. Blake would under-tand and agree. Surely he didn't want to complicate their vorking relationship. It had been a one-time misstep, incon-gruous and regrettable, and never to be repeated.

The baby in her arms was stirring back to full wakeful-ess. She carried him upstairs and found a large bedroom vith pale blue walls, decorated with sailboats and furnished vith a dark cherry crib, dresser and changing table. The last ime she'd been here, the room had just been finished. The tuffed animals that now filled the window seat that over-ooked the ocean hadn't been here. There'd been no baskets n the floor filled with stacking cups and electronic games. No well-worn books had filled the shelves.

Now the space looked lived-in. Loved.

Bella set Drew on the floor near the basket of toys and egan unpacking his clothes. A fire truck with a siren held his attention for as long as it took Bella to fill one drawer. After that he crawled to the low bookcase and began pulling out one story after another. Seeing the mess he was making, Bella left the rest of the unpacking for later and joined him on the floor.

"What should we read first?" She scanned the books.

"He's particularly fond of *Belly Button Book*," Blake said from the doorway.

Bella located the story and turned to thank him for the suggestion, but the words faltered on her lips at the sight of him in khakis, a white polo shirt and navy blazer. The casual clothes reminded her of those days last summer when they'd sat on the back porch and he'd told her about his favorite places in the Virgin Islands and about how he'd first tried *cinghiale*—wild boar—in a small village in Tuscany. She'd been surprised to learn that they hunted wild boar in Italy and that it was a favorite dish in the region.

He'd opened her eyes to adventures she'd never imagined when she'd been growing up on a small farm in Iowa and her dreams had expanded to include traveling beyond the borders of the U.S.

"I should be back in time to put him to bed," Blake told her.

"Don't feel the need to rush back. We'll be just fine." She lifted the baby onto her lap and opened the book. "Enjoy your dinner."

"Thank you," Blake said.

It wasn't until he was gone that Bella realized she'd been holding her breath. She released the air in a gusty sigh and kissed Drew on top of his head. "That daddy of yours sure ties me in knots," she confided to the baby. "Did you see the way he kissed me this afternoon?"

Drew smacked the book with his hands and made impatient noises.

"Typical guy," Bella teased. "When it comes to talking

about feelings, you aren't interested in hearing what a woman has to say."

And without further delay, she began to read.

Five

Blake cursed as he turned into the driveway of the house Jeanne and Peter had rented and spied three cars parked in front. His stepsister had lied to him. This wasn't a quiet family dinner. It was a setup.

One of her numerous socialite friends from New York? An oil baron's daughter from Texas? Hopefully she hadn't fixed him up with the actress from Los Angeles she'd met the previous week. The possibilities were endless, considering Jeanne's vast social connections and vivacious personality.

"Blake." Jeanne flung open the door before he had a chance to ring the bell. "I'm so glad you could join us." She grabbed his arm and pulled him toward the living room.

Her over-the-top gaiety deepened Blake's suspicions. She was trying too hard.

Peter met him in the living room doorway and handed him a cut-crystal tumbler with a three-finger shot of whiskey. "I told her this was a bad idea."

Blake's chest vibrated with a suppressed growl. "Jeanne, what's going on?"

He loved his stepsister, but sometimes she didn't know when to stop her well-meaning machinations. She liked the world organized to her specific standards. And most of the time she got her way.

"Look who was able to get away from New York to join us for the weekend." Jeanne maneuvered him around Peter and into the contemporary monstrosity of a living room where Blake's ex-wife stood, her expression a mask of delight, her eyes flaring defiance.

"Damn it, Jeanne," he began, biting off the rest of the sentence when his stepsister gripped his hand hard.

"Don't be mad. You two are my favorite people in the world." Her husband made a disgusted sound behind her that she ignored. "I can't have you refusing to be in the same room. There's going to be harmony in this house when the baby comes." Her lovely features wore the determined expression they all knew too well. "I mean it."

Blake took a healthy swallow of his drink and relished the burn in his throat and chest. He concentrated on getting a handle on his annoyance before he spoke. "So, this isn't a setup?" He thought he sounded cool and relaxed, but Peter winced, Jeanne's eyes went wide and Vicky grew pale.

"Must you suspect everyone's motives?"

"Not everyone's," he retorted smoothly, saluting his stepsister with the glass. "Just yours."

Jeanne rolled her shoulders in an elegant shrug and nudged him toward Vicky. "Go be nice while I have Peter refresh your drink."

Tension marred his ex-wife's lovely features as he approached her. Stunning in a figure-hugging black dress that showed off a significant amount of cleavage, she'd obviously spent a great deal of time on her hair and makeup. If she was hoping he'd be moved that she'd gone to so much trouble for him, she was destined for disappointment.

"I don't need to ask how you've been," she murmured. "You look wonderful."

"Fatherhood agrees with me."

"I knew it would."

The flow of conversation was interrupted when Peter handed him a tumbler of scotch. When they began again, Vicky changed the topic to recent gossip about their friends. She didn't ask after Drew. Eight months ago this would have annoyed Blake. In the months since she'd left, he'd grudgingly accepted that he'd been too blinded by his desire to be a parent to realize his wife didn't share his enthusiasm. In the week after they'd brought their son home from the hospital, Vicky hadn't held the baby more than a half dozen times, each for less than ten minutes. Pity he hadn't recognized her lack of maternal instinct earlier. It would have saved them both a great deal of heartache.

"I heard that your play closed," he said. "I'm sorry to hear it didn't work out."

She shrugged. "There will be others."

Blake spied telltale signs of anxiety in the lines bracketing her mouth. "I thought you were very good."

"You saw it?"

"Of course. Don't sound so surprised. You know I've always been your biggest fan."

News of her affair had left him angry and raw for twenty-four hours. It had taken him that long to process the abrupt end of his five-year marriage and to remember that his energy was better spent caring for his son.

"But I thought…" She looked baffled.

"That I hated you?" He shook his head. "We wanted different things. You, a career. Me, a family. I didn't appreciate the way you ended things, but I've been told that I can be a bit difficult to say no to." He snagged her gaze and let his lips drift into a conciliatory curve.

"That's so reasonable of you." Her tone reflected doubt.

"I told you fatherhood agrees with me."

"I guess it does."

"Drew's terrific. Stop by the house anytime if you'd like to see him." He made the offer knowing she'd never do that.

"I will." She nodded. "I'm heading to Los Angeles next week. Maybe we could have lunch at the Saw Grass Grill before I leave?"

The restaurant where they'd agreed to start a family. Had she been honest in her agreement, or had it merely been a way to preserve their marriage? He'd never be sure whether what she'd told him was the truth or merely what she'd believed he wanted to hear. One thing he did know, he'd missed all the warning signs that Vicky wasn't interested in being a mother.

He was saved from having to answer by the arrival of the housekeeper announcing dinner was ready. Blake lingered in the living room while the other three made their way into the dining room. Blake wasn't surprised to see that Jeanne had placed him next to Victoria to suit her matchmaking scheme.

His sister wasn't behaving as if she'd listened when he told her he intended to put his son's needs first. Of course, he wasn't exactly walking the walk either. Kissing Bella this afternoon had been a mistake. There was no denying he wanted her, but she was far too determined to remain childless. Getting involved with her was contrary to everything he wanted for Drew. Better to heed her warning. Pursuing her would complicate things between them and he needed their relationship to be trouble free, for Drew's sake.

That decided, he returned his attention to the dinner conversation, ignoring the burn of disappointment in his gut.

* * *

Bella stared down at a sleeping Drew, unable to obey the logical side of her brain that told her to grab the baby monitor and go. She needed to remember that Drew was nothing more than a job. She was his nanny. This tightness in her chest would go away the instant she accepted that Drew belonged to Blake and only Blake. She had no claim on him. No reason to ache for all the firsts she'd already missed and all the ones still to come that she wouldn't get to experience.

Damn Blake. It was all his fault. First he'd tracked her down. Then he'd offered her the financial means to help her sister and not feel guilty for spending money on a fabulous trip to the Caribbean. If not for him, she might be broke and resentful, but she'd be blissfully free of the emotional chaos churning in her gut. Free of the anxiety that came with being responsible for another human being.

Reaching down, she grazed her knuckles across Drew's soft cheek. This afternoon when he'd been stung, she'd longed to take on his pain as her own. She hadn't been able to separate herself from his hurt the way she did when something harmed her brothers and sisters. It was as if despite being apart for nine months, she and Drew shared a bond. He would always be hers no matter how many miles separated them.

It was a disquieting thought that she wished she could unthink.

Her phone buzzed in her back pocket, alerting her that a text had come in. She suspected that it was Blake checking in again, so relief surged through her when she saw Deidre's name on the display. Bella exited the nursery, pulling the door closed behind her, and went to sit on the steps that descended toward the darkened first floor. She keyed up her friend's message and grimaced at the video of Deidre dancing with three guys.

There's too many gorgeous guys for me to keep happy all by myself.

That could be her. Young, single and ready to break hearts all over town. No responsibilities. No worries. Just fun.

Bella texted her friend back.

I've seen you in action and have faith that you can do it.

A minute later her phone rang.

"We miss you." Deidre's fervent voice sounded loud in the still house as she made it sound like Bella had been gone for weeks instead of hours.

"I miss you, too."

"How are things there?" From the background noise, it sounded like Deidre was in the ladies' room.

Bella waffled over how much to tell her friend and finally decided to ease into it. "A little weird."

"Weird how?"

"You were right about Blake."

"Aha!" Deidre crowed. A second later her voice quieted. Tension gathered in her tone. "What do you mean I was right?"

"He kissed me." A stunned silence followed Bella's declaration. With her nerves frayed by too much self-doubt, Bella wished her friend would say something. She could really use Deidre's sensible council. "Did you hear me?"

"I did. I'm just trying to figure out how to respond." Another pause. "Yippee?"

"No, not yippee," Bella shot back. "Yikes."

Deidre laughed. "Yikes, indeed. Boy, does he work fast. What sort of a kiss was it?"

"What do you mean, what sort of a kiss?"

"Friendly? Some people kiss on the lips to say hello or goodbye. Was it that sort of a kiss?"

Despite the hysteria bubbling up, Bella appreciated her roommate's matter-of-fact way of assessing the situation.

"No. It was not a friendly kiss."

"Juicy, then." Deidre's voice barely missed sounding like a triumphant whoop. "Did he rock your world?"

The question aroused an untimely urge to giggle. "He does that just by walking in the room."

"You've got it worse than I thought."

"So much worse." Bella set her forehead on her knees and cradled the phone against her ear. "I keep telling myself it was just a one-time thing and it won't happen again."

"Is that what you believe?"

"No." Hot flashes surged through Bella's body. "What should I do?"

"You're asking the wrong girl. I'd sleep with him in a New York minute. He's gorgeous and sexy. Nothing wrong with two single people enjoying each other's company. But that's me. What do you want to do?"

Bella had never been able to cultivate Deidre's casual attitude toward sex. As much as she'd love to be a sophisticated woman taking large bites out of the Big Apple, in truth, she was still a girl who'd grown up on a farm in Iowa. Granted, she didn't want to get married and start a family, but that didn't mean that she could see herself jumping into bed with someone where there was no possibility of a future.

"What I want to do goes against my nature."

"Bella, you've been stuck on this guy way too long. Offer him a couple months of uncomplicated sex and get him out of your system." Voices called Deidre's name from somewhere close by. "I have to go. Call me tomorrow and we'll talk more about this."

"I will. Have fun tonight."

Without Deidre's vibrant voice filling her ear, Bella's anxiety returned in spades. It was crazy to contemplate what could happen with Blake. She'd already decided against repeating this afternoon's kiss. It would be easier on her heart that way.

Beside her Drew's baby monitor picked up a soft cry. Blake had warned her that he'd been having trouble staying asleep lately and she wondered at the source of his restlessness. Was he cutting new teeth? The discomfort of that had kept her youngest sister up nights for two solid months.

Drew quieted before Bella could stand. Ears keyed to the tiniest noise, she heard the sound of approaching footsteps from below. Blake was back earlier than she expected. And he was humming. What had put him in such a good mood?

"How was your evening?" she asked as he rounded the landing.

His eyes lit up as he spied her sitting on the steps. "Waiting up for me?"

"No." The last thing she needed was for him to think she'd spent the evening missing him. "I just got off the phone with my friend. She couldn't wait to tell me how much fun she was having at this new club."

Blake stretched out on the stair beside her. His knee bumped her thigh. The casual contact zinged through her body. Shifting away would betray her agitation. Holding still took all her concentration.

"Wish you were there?" A lazy smile appeared on his well-formed lips, but the eyes that surveyed her were keen and curious.

"A little."

She tried to keep her eyes off him, but the dim stairwell offered little of interest to distract her. And there was a whole lot of wonderful occupying far too much of her personal space. In complete contrast to her tense muscles, he looked entirely at ease beside her. His elbow rested on the top step, fingers interlocked loosely. Beneath his navy blazer, a white shirt stretched across his broad chest, the top button undone to reveal the strong column of his throat.

He was strong, masculine, utterly confident in every situation, and Bella could feature him in a hundred fantasies without taxing her imagination. Deidre was right. She'd been hung up on Blake for too long. But was a brief, casual affair the best way to get him out of her system?

"Tomorrow night I'll stay home with Drew," he offered. "You can go out and have some fun of your own."

"By myself?" She didn't mean for the question to come out sounding as grim as it did, and Blake's eyes brimmed with amusement. "What I mean is I don't know anyone here. I'm not sure I want to go to a bar alone."

"I'll get Jeanne to watch Drew and I'll take you."

His offer made her pulse race. She imagined herself in a bar with Blake. A glass of wine to relax her. The throb of electronic music making her blood run hot. How long before she dragged him onto the crowded dance floor and gave in to the hunger he aroused?

"That's nice of you to suggest, but I don't think you and I going out is a good idea."

Her repressive manner put him on instant alert. He regarded her through narrowed eyes for a long moment before asking, "Any reason why not?"

"I've been doing some thinking since earlier."

"About what?"

"About what happened between us today."

His lips arced in a predatory smile. "I've been thinking about it, as well."

"Then you'll agree that it was a mistake."

"I can't say that."

His declaration gave Bella pause. This was not going as planned. "I'm your son's nanny."

"If you're worried that things will become uncomfortable between us, I have no intention of letting that happen."

She relaxed. "Good. I think it's for the best if nothing further happens."

"I truly wish I could make that promise." Blake's exhalation sounded weary. "Earlier tonight, I thought I could. But now I realize I can't."

"Why not?" Her voice pitched higher than normal as she asked the question.

"Because it's not that easy to keep my hands off you."

Six

Sitting on the steps was not an ideal place to begin a seduction, but Blake wasn't about to risk Bella bolting for the safety of her bedroom if he let her get to her feet. Her resistance amused him. It was as if all her arguing against an affair between them was aimed at convincing herself. He was confident she wanted him. He just needed her to admit it.

He cupped her neck to hold her still while he slid his lips into the hollow above her collarbone. The contact made her shiver. Her skin was warm silk. Softer than he'd expected. He pulled in a long, slow breath, taking in the scent of her. Vanilla and jasmine. Simple fragrances for an uncomplicated woman.

"Blake—" She whispered his name, objecting even as she leaned into his searching lips.

"Yes, Bella?" He sampled more of her skin, grazing his mouth up her neck. Her soft sigh made him smile in satisfaction.

"We really shouldn't."

"Are you telling me to stop?" Instead of waiting for her to answer, he let his fingertips slip from her neck to her shoulder, drawing her into his space. He wanted to overwhelm her with intent. Compel her understanding. He wanted her. Very much. "Just say stop. I'll quit."

His teeth grazed her throat. She moaned something, but the word that left her lips wasn't *stop*. Her fingers bit into his shoulders. He felt their fierce hold through his blazer. For a woman who wanted him to believe she was opposed to letting the chemistry between them run its course, she was not resisting.

"Let's go." Suddenly impatient, he got to his feet and swept her into his arms.

She looked dazed for a moment, but as he strode toward his bedroom, her eyes cleared. "Go where?"

"I'm going to make love to you, Bella."

Her big blue eyes regarded him in consternation. "I don't want that."

He set her on her feet in the doorway to his bedroom, but didn't dare set her free. "Then we'll only do as much as you do want."

"You'll stop?"

"Whenever you say." His finger found her chin and elevated it until her face was at a perfect angle. He placed his lips on hers in a gentle kiss meant to reassure her. The tension humming in her muscles eased slightly, so he set his palm against her spine and drew her ever so slowly against him.

Her breath quickened as their hips came together. Restraint came at a price as her hands slid beneath his jacket. Fingers fanning over his rib cage, she took the kiss up a notch, parting her lips and flicking her tongue across his teeth. He let her in, captured her breath in his lungs and held it while she grew bolder.

Sliding one foot between hers, he backed her against the

doorframe. Her surprised inhalation barely registered as he pressed his thigh against the heat of her core. They rocked together in a languid rhythm, matched by the dueling feint and retreat of their tongues. Keenly focused on her every sigh and the trembling of her body, he was rapidly losing faith that if she asked him to stop he could.

"Do you want to stop?" he questioned, sliding his fingers beneath her simple T-shirt. Her skin was impossibly hot, as if she was on fire for him.

The modest neckline had gaped when he'd lifted her into his arms, offering him a peek at her flesh-colored bra. So practical. Nothing seductive about it. Yet he couldn't wait to see her in it.

She pushed him to arm's length. "I think we should."

Gusting out a sigh, Blake stepped back. As his hands fell to his side, she studied him.

"As you wish."

"That's just it, don't you see?" Her expression reflected frustration. "I don't want to stop. I want to keep going. Until we're naked and rolling around in that big bed over there." She gestured to where his king-size bed sat between two patches of moonlight. "But I think that would be a huge mistake."

Her breath rasped, the cadence agitated. Blake wanted to snatch her into his arms and kiss away all her angst. With her eyes glowing, her mouth soft from his kisses, she was spectacular. And worth waiting for.

He took her hands and turned her palms upward. Bending, he placed a kiss in each one. "It's late. Why don't we call it a night?"

"You've changed your mind?" She sounded heartbroken. "Just like that?"

"You said stop."

She yanked her hands free. "I didn't say stop. I simply said it would be a mistake."

Her logic escaped him. "How is that different than stop?"

"You are so exasperating."

Before he had a clue to her intentions, she'd stripped her shirt over her head and eliminated the distance between them. He had about a second to appreciate the curves of her breasts before they slammed into his chest.

His arms came about her, binding her to him. She was silk and fire in his grasp. With a low groan, Blake dropped his mouth onto hers and found her lips parted in invitation. Any hesitation she might have demonstrated these past ten minutes was lost in the heat of her ardent response to his kiss.

Taking things slowly—savoring her surrender—was proving difficult. While their mouths melded in passionate harmony, in the back of his mind he braced for her doubts to resurface. They didn't. Once committed, she was a siren calling him to lose all touch with reality and follow her anywhere.

Chest heaving, Blake eased back. As much as he hated to risk giving her time to come to her senses, standing in his doorway was an awkward place to romance her properly. Her eyes were heavy lidded and slightly unfocused as he led her toward the bed.

In a flash he'd stripped off his blazer and pulled his shirt over his head. She gazed at his chest in fascination. He flinched as her fingertips settled on his skin.

"You acted as if that hurt," she said, absorbed in her study of his bare chest.

"Your touch has a strong effect on me."

"It does?" She traced his pectoral muscles, fascinated by every curve she encountered. "Is that good or bad?"

"It's very good." Although he was dying to let his own fingers do some exploring, he kept his hands on her hips. He would have all night to discover her body. "I like being touched by you."

Her smile came and went. "You are as beautiful as I imagined." Did she realize what she'd let slip?

"My turn." He guided her onto the mattress and followed her down, his lips drifting along her throat and across her chest to the edge of her bra. "You are perfect."

She squirmed beneath him as he grazed her nipple through the fabric of her bra. "That feels amazing." Reaching behind her, she unfastened the catch. With a quick jerk, she freed herself from the bra and tossed it aside. "This will be even better."

Blake groaned as he closed his mouth around one tight bud. He laved her with his tongue and then sucked until she arched off the mattress. Whimpering, she clutched at his hair. Never had he been with a woman as sensitive as Bella. Suddenly he was hungry for more. He blazed a trail down her stomach. Unzipping her pants took only a second. With fingers that trembled, he hooked her waistband and slid the fabric down her thighs. She lifted her hips to aid him and in no time she lay in the middle of his bed clad in nothing but her panties.

It was a moment worth appreciating, and Blake was a man who knew the value of doing so. First with his gaze, then with his hands, he learned the arch of her feet, the slenderness of her ankles, the muscular thrust of her calves, the lean length of her thighs, the flare of her hips and flatness of her abdomen. He lingered over each ripple in her rib cage, drawing out the suspense until his fingers circled her breasts.

When she grabbed his hands and cupped them over her breasts, Blake knew she'd suffered all she could take. Leaning down, he captured her mouth, branding her with a sizzling kiss.

Bella had never felt anything like Blake's hands on her body. He paid attention to every inch of her skin, as if he wanted to know all of her, not just the "good parts." It made her feel adored, something she'd never known before.

The crushing weight of his body lifted off her as he abandoned her mouth to blaze a trail of delicious sensation down her body. Expecting he would turn his attention back to her breasts, she was disappointed when he paused only long enough to draw a wet circle around one nipple before following her ribs downward. He lingered on her abdomen, dipping his tongue into her navel and awakening a series of shudders. By the time his lips drifted over her hip bone, Bella was half-mad with wanting.

Her thighs had parted ages ago. Between them she throbbed with increasing hunger. She craved his hard length buried inside her. The need grew with each circle of his tongue and press of his lips against her feverish skin. But it wasn't until his broad shoulders nudged her legs wide did she awaken to what he intended.

She gasped. "Blake."

He looked up at her call. His chin bumped against her hot core, sending a spear of pleasure lancing through her. Her breath suspended as their gazes locked.

"Are you asking me to stop?" he challenged, letting his lips drift over her mound.

Stop? Was he mad?

The slight tug of fabric against her sensitized flesh rendered her incoherent. If it was like this before his lips found her bare skin, what would it be like when he'd stripped away the last of her clothes?

"It's…"

She broke off as he trailed his tongue along the edge of her panties. Sliding his hands down her legs, he gripped her behind the thighs and bent her knees until her feet were flat on the mattress. Every movement caused an escalation in the commotion inside her. Her fingers gripped the sheet beneath her. She'd never had anyone kiss her there.

"I'll go slowly," he told her, capturing her gaze. "You tell me when to stop."

Stop?

It was glorious to watch his pleasure in her body's every reaction. How could she possibly stop him from indulging his power over her? Helplessly, she waited, her breath shallow and ragged as his warm breath washed over her. And then he pressed a kiss there and a strangled groan broke from her throat. She was lost as the bold stroke of his tongue licked over her. Her hips bucked. A wild laugh erupted from her tight chest.

"Stop?" He ceased all movement.

She wanted to weep with longing. "Don't…"

"More?"

Amusement edged his tone. Part of her recognized she should be angry with him for taunting her, but she was on the edge of something glorious and devastating.

"Yes."

"It would be easier if I took these off." He hooked his fingers in her panties and tugged.

She lifted her hips. "Do it."

The fabric skimmed off her body far too slowly. Bella's head thrashed from side to side as she felt the air hit her overheated flesh. With her eyes closed, it felt safer. She could pretend it was anyone between her thighs, but the second Blake spoke, she became grounded in the moment once more.

"I'm going to kiss you now." But he didn't immediately follow through with his promise. Bella's heart thumped hard against her ribs as she waited. "Care to watch?"

Enticed by the question, her lashes drifted upward. He was waiting for her. He wanted her to see what he intended to do. Bella shuddered at the intensity in his eyes, but couldn't look away as his tongue stroked against her.

She cried out, an incoherent sound barely loud enough to escape the confines of the bed. Blake's gaze electrified her. His kiss set her ablaze. He was thorough. Each wet circle of his tongue sent her spiraling higher. The ache in her belly coiled into a tight knot. Her world shrank to the feel of Blake's mouth on her and the rapid approach of cresting pleasure.

Her hips rose off the mattress, frantically searching for the fulfillment that eluded her. She was whimpering, her breath coming in erratic and short bursts.

"Let go," he urged. "Come for me."

And then she felt the slide of his finger inside her. The penetration touched off her orgasm and her spine bowed as she exploded like a firework, splintering into a million hot shards before returning to earth in a gentle waterfall.

Bella's cries were the sweetest music Blake had ever heard. Beneath him she continued to tremble in the aftermath of her powerful orgasm. At long last her lashes fluttered and her gaze focused on him. There was such wonder in the much-washed blue of her eyes. Blake's heart clenched.

"That was amazing," she murmured.

He kissed his way up her body until he reached her mouth. "There's more to come," he murmured against her lips.

Bella coasted her fingertips over his lower lip before settling her palm against his cheek. Her gentle touch was as much about claiming him as surrendering to his will.

"I'm glad."

Moving quickly, he stripped off his pants and rolled on a condom. Her arms came around him as he rejoined her on the bed. Where a second earlier her body had been limp and sated, as he positioned himself between her thighs and sucked her nipple between his lips, she became a living flame once more. Her fingers wandered across his shoulders and down his spine. The scratch of her nails along his sides startled him.

Before he could ask her if she wanted to stop, she spoke.

"Enough with the preliminaries. I need to feel you inside me."

She bumped her hips upward, nudging his erection and making him quake with yearning. Never one to keep a woman waiting, he positioned himself at her entrance and claimed her mouth in a long, deep kiss. Then he thrust gently. She was so wet and aroused that he was nearly seated all the way in before he stopped himself. After a brief pause to gather much-needed air, he began moving with a smooth rocking motion that she matched as fluidly as if they'd made love a thousand times.

The ease of their connection caught Blake by surprise. It occurred to him that he knew Bella well and at the same time didn't know her at all. From the first she'd intrigued him. Later, her contrary behavior had frustrated him. There was so much yet to discover about her. So many unanswered questions. And he would have most of the summer to ferret them out.

"Blake." Her clutching fingers told him she was close to another climax.

He'd been distracting his mind to prolong their encounter, but as her nails dug into his back and her cries grew more frantic, Blake loosened the hold on his willpower and thrust powerfully into her. Capturing her pleasure in a hot, demanding kiss, he slipped his hand between their bodies and touched the knot of nerves that would send her spinning into another orgasm.

As her body contracted, he let his own climax catch him. With a final thrust, he buried his face in her neck and gave her everything. Shuddering, his arm muscles unable to support him any longer, he collapsed on her.

"Now, that was amazing," he said, chest heaving as he struggled to recover.

Eyes glowing with contentment, Bella parted her lips to respond, but before she could, a cry erupted from beyond the room. Recognizing the quality of the cry, Blake nevertheless willed his son back to sleep. It was a fruitless proposition.

Another unhappy wail filtered in from the nursery, this one of longer duration than the last. Drew didn't sound as if he was going to settle down on his own.

Blake put his forehead against Bella's shoulder and heaved a sigh. "I'd better get him."

"Let me."

With an abrupt shake of his head, Blake pushed away from her warm, silken skin, grinding his teeth as he was pummeled by the room's cool air. "I've been through this with him. I'll have an easier time getting him back to sleep." He covered her with the sheet and bent down to buss her cheek. "Sleep."

"Sure." She gave him an uncertain smile.

Blake's movements felt jerky and uncoordinated as he slid back into his clothes. His muscles hadn't fully recovered from the mind-blowing sex with Bella. He cast a final look her way before he headed for the doorway. What he saw gave him pause.

If not for his son's escalating distress, Blake would have lingered to reassure Bella that he too had been affected by the power of what had happened between them. The last thing he wanted with any woman was to take her to a vulnerable place and abandon her there. He sensed Bella wasn't the sort of woman who took sex lightly.

Which meant leaving her so soon after being intimate would undo some of the rapport they'd established. She'd had her doubts earlier, but he'd been able to reassure her. Abandoning her in his bed would give her ample time to re-establish her defenses.

But there was nothing to do about that. His son needed him. It was something Bella understood. She'd often put her family's needs above her own; it was a big part of what appealed to him about her. On the other hand, when she'd decided to cut off all ties with Drew, she'd demonstrated that like his ex-wife, she had a selfish side.

And what of his decision a mere three hours ago not to complicate their relationship by acting on his desire for her? He certainly hadn't been thinking about what was best for his son while he made love to her. What he needed was a mother for Drew. Bella wasn't interested in the role.

So why had he felt compelled to have her spend part of the summer with them? Had he hoped if she spent time with Drew her maternal instincts would awaken?

When he got to the nursery, Blake lifted his son into his arms and rocked him the way he knew Drew loved. Almost immediately the infant's cries waned. He met Drew's eyes and felt peace wash through him. He wanted the world for his son, but right now he would settle for a mother who would love him with her whole heart.

Which was why making love to Bella tonight had been a mistake. They could no longer pretend to be simply boss and employee. But he couldn't promise to keep his hands off her in the future. He'd told Jeanne he intended to put Drew first the next time he married. Getting involved with a woman who didn't want to be a mother ran contrary to that determination. But being with her felt so right. What the hell was he supposed to do?

Seven

Abandoned in Blake's enormous bed, Bella pressed a pillow against her stomach and curved her naked body around it, coiling herself into a tight ball. The instant he'd left the room, her sense of belonging had vanished with him.

Earlier, while Blake was dining with his stepsister, she'd glanced into the master bedroom. Residual traces of Victoria—like the photographs in the living room—lingered in the large, beautifully decorated space. Blake's ex-wife remained a presence in the house, and Bella felt like an imposter. An interloper. Had she really just made love to Blake?

The riotous sensations still buffeting her body as well as the residual tingle left behind by the imprint of Blake's lips told her she had stepped across a line. And now that she'd left footprints in forbidden territory, there was no taking it back. But was that what she wanted? To unmake the memories of the past hour?

Bella rubbed her hot cheeks against the cool sheets. Nothing could have prepared her for the explosive quality of Blake's mouth on her body. The things he'd done. No one had ever kissed her like that before. Done things to her body that made her go wild. To say they were unmatched in experience was woefully inadequate. She'd had so much to learn. Tonight it had been all she could do just to hang on for dear life as he took her on an epic ride. In the aftermath, she recognized that a man as sophisticated as Blake would expect his lover to match him in skill and knowledge.

Through the door Blake had closed behind him, Bella could hear Drew's continuing cries. The instinct to go to him thundered through her. He was her baby. Comforting him was her job. Her responsibility.

Except that it wasn't. Drew belonged to Blake. And in a way, to Victoria. She might have abandoned him, but as far as the world knew, Blake's ex-wife was his mother. Bella was just someone who'd acted as a surrogate. A living incubator. Well paid and insignificant the second Drew was born.

But his cries tore at her. No matter how hard she tried to be sensible, the need to cuddle him until his tears dried up was so much more compelling than her desire to be free of responsibility. The war between her brain and her emotions was leaving her confidence in tatters. Her doubts about the choices she'd made about Drew were growing stronger day by day.

As Bella threw back the covers, the house went silent. She held her breath, waiting for the cries to start again, but no sound stirred. Far from anything resembling sleepiness, Bella dressed and eased out of the room. Drew's door was shut, but a faint light glimmered beneath. Tiptoeing forward, she drew close and heard Blake's deep voice. He was telling Drew a story, his tone pitched to engage an infant.

Reluctant to enter the nursery and disturb what Blake had accomplished, Bella retreated toward her room, but instead of heading inside, she took the stairs to the first floor. In bare feet she was able to move soundlessly across the polished wood floor of the living room. Drawn by the light of the moon, she crossed to the windows that overlooked the ocean. Snagging a throw from a nearby chair, she wrapped it around her shoulders before letting herself out the door.

A wide porch stretched across the back half of the house, offering a place to rest and enjoy the view. White wood lounge chairs covered with thick, cobalt-blue cushions were scattered here and there. Straight ahead a wide set of steps led to an expansive lawn. At the far end, a boardwalk split the vegetation capping the low dunes lining the beach. A light wind carried the sound of the surf to Bella's ears. She headed down the steps and across the lawn.

From her first glimpse at the ocean last summer, it had been love at first sight. Everything about the beach had fascinated her, from the birds to the myriad of trinkets left behind by the tide to the pulse of the ocean itself. With her toes gripping the sand, she'd stared at the horizon and pulled the briny air into her lungs, letting the sights, sounds and smells fill her with peace.

She'd been close to her due date and riddled with doubts that she was doing the right thing by herself and her son. She'd hoped that spending a couple weeks with Blake and Victoria and seeing their eagerness to be parents would enable her to set aside her misgivings. The beach had settled her anxiety and allowed her to gain perspective.

By the end of the first week, she'd accepted that the baby she carried would be brought up by loving parents who could provide everything he could ever want or need. At peace with her decision to help Blake and Victoria, she'd given birth to Drew and walked out of the hospital, never imagining that she'd see him again.

Yet here she was nine months later, taking care of Drew once more, pretending that a conflict wasn't raging inside her. Once again grappling to make sense of what her heart wanted versus what she believed would make her happy. In the long run she knew being a mom would only make her resentful, yet every fiber of her being longed for Drew. And after what had happened between her and Blake tonight, she yearned for him, as well.

It would be so easy to surrender her heart to them. Equal parts charming and aggravating, they'd slipped beneath her skin in a disturbingly short period of time. She had no trouble imagining herself becoming a part of their lives. Taking care of them. Falling into a routine that would leave little time or energy for the things she wanted.

Bella retraced her steps to the house. Earlier tonight she'd discovered the power Blake held over her. She'd been disappointed they'd had no chance to cement the connection they'd forged during their lovemaking, but relieved for the opportunity to gain perspective before facing Blake again.

Not one thing she'd experienced tonight had left her unaffected. Should she get out before it was too late? She could tell Blake she'd changed her mind. It wasn't too late to back away from the edge.

And never make love to him? Her body ached at the thought.

Bella stopped halfway across the lawn and faced the ocean. Lifting her face to the wind, she quieted her mind and listened for the truth.

In the past two years she'd learned a great deal about herself. She'd reimagined her dreams. She'd learned more about her strengths and desires. And she'd enjoy her time with Blake as long as it lasted. A day, a week or a month. Whatever she could have. If she was smart and kept her head on straight, she could do exactly as Deidre suggested and enjoy his company for as long as it lasted.

When it was done, they would part friends.

With Victoria and Blake's marriage over, it was no longer necessary for Bella to keep away from Drew. But what sort of relationship did she want with him? Back when she'd given birth, Blake had expected her to stay in touch. Come to Drew's birthday parties. Join them for dinner. Take him to the park. She would have been a family friend, an honorary aunt. That had been her intention until Victoria had asked her to stay away.

But Victoria was no longer in the picture. She'd chosen her career over her son. Rejected the baby that was supposed to keep her marriage together. Now the only women in Drew's life were his nanny and Blake's stepsister. And with Jeanne expecting a child of her own, how much time would she have to spend with Drew?

Bella could fill in here and there, but Drew deserved a full-time mother. Soon Blake would get past any lingering feelings of distrust left over from Victoria's duplicity and remarry. That would leave Bella on the outside looking in again.

Which shouldn't bother her. She didn't want the responsibility of a child. But she didn't like being an outsider looking in on her son's life, either. As hard as it had been to cut all ties, each day she'd missed Drew a little less. Who knew—in a year or ten, she might have forgotten all about Blake and Drew if he had never found her at St. Vincent's.

Bella laughed bitterly at her foolishness and lifted her face to the wind. The brine from the ocean mingled with the salt of her tears.

Instead, in less than three days, she'd made memories that would haunt her to her dying day.

Like the master bedroom, the nursery faced the back of the house. Blake stood before the large picture window, one hand on his son's crib, and watched Bella return from the beach. Their lovemaking had been spectacular. Bella's innocence refreshing. Her enthusiasm addictive. The play of emotion on her face fascinating. When he'd set his mouth on her, she'd been surprised. Shocked, even. Discovering each thing that pleasured her made him feverish to learn more. How many things could he introduce her to? The possibilities appeared to be endless.

The moon was three-quarters full and high overhead, providing enough light for him to follow the lone figure as she made her way across the lawn. Despite the distance between them, Blake could see the determined set of her shoulders. She strode toward the house as if marching into battle. What a fascinating woman she was. A perplexing blend of determination and insecurity, as if she knew what she wanted, but was afraid to grab it with both hands.

And tonight she'd wanted him. Her boldness had been a delightful surprise. After the way she'd pushed him away this afternoon, he'd assumed he'd spend the next week convincing her to fall into his arms. He'd never expected she'd arrive at the decision all on her own.

Not that he believed for one second that what had happened between them earlier meant that their relationship would proceed smoothly. Jeanne's presence down the road and her goal of reuniting him with Victoria was a complication that wouldn't just go away. If his stepsister had any inkling of what he intended for Bella, she would move heaven and earth to stop him.

The muffled sound of a closing door roused him out of his thoughts. Bella had returned to her room, not to his. As tempting as it was to follow her and resume what Drew had interrupted, Blake stayed put.

Earlier that evening he'd reaffirmed that he intended to put Drew's needs before his own, and what his son required was a mother. So what was he doing with Bella? He couldn't see their relationship going anywhere, because Bella wasn't interested in being a part of the sort of family he wanted. One night of sex, no matter how amazing, wasn't going to change her mind on that score.

But as he'd slipped between her thighs and claimed her

as his, he hadn't been thinking about convincing her how wonderful it would be for her to take on the role of Drew's mother. He hadn't been thinking at all. He'd been feeling. Desire. Possessiveness. Pleasure.

He'd stormed past her defenses. Made her surrender. Claimed her in the most elemental way possible. He'd been careful, used a condom, but he was spellbound by the compelling fantasy of her big and round with another child, this one theirs alone, created in the throes of passion.

Last time he hadn't been able to share the experience with her the way he now wanted to. To feel his child move inside her. To indulge her every craving. To observe every miraculous change in her body.

He wanted what was best for his son, but couldn't deny his longing for many more sensational nights with Bella. The dilemma haunted him long into the night.

Tired and grouchy from lack of sleep, Blake woke the next morning at eight and went to check on Drew, only to discover both he and Bella were nowhere to be found.

Mrs. Farnes had breakfast waiting for him when he entered the kitchen. Beyond the sliding glass door that led out to the side yard, sunshine spilled across the large patio where he'd had an outdoor kitchen installed. Victoria had enjoyed entertaining. They threw two large parties every summer to raise money for some charity or another and her birthday party in July was always an elaborate affair.

His ex-wife liked being the center of attention, and Blake had indulged her need to be adored.

Life with Bella would be quieter. He wouldn't be expected to entertain people he scarcely knew and barely liked after spending a long week at the office. The relief of it hit him square in the forehead. Until this moment, he hadn't realized how much he'd craved a weekend alone with his wife when they were still together.

"Have you seen Bella and Drew this morning?"

"She took him for a run."

He had no idea she jogged. The last time she'd stayed at the beach house, she'd been eight months pregnant and moving no faster than a swift waddle.

How many other things were there about her that he didn't know?

"Any idea when they'll be back?"

"She said she intended to go five miles and they've been gone forty-five minutes. Do you want breakfast now or did you want to wait and eat with them?"

"I'll take the paper and a cup of coffee for now and eat later."

His study was at the back of the house, overlooking the formal gardens. On cool mornings like this, he enjoyed opening the windows to take in the tantalizing scent of roses. As he crossed the foyer, the front door opened and a flushed, animated Bella pushed a jogging stroller inside. She wore thin black shorts and a snug hot pink tank top that showed off her lean form.

Blake's gaze slid over her in appreciation. She was sporting a sassy high ponytail that drew attention to her heart-shaped face and expressive blue eyes. As soon as she spotted him, her expression brightened even more.

"What a gorgeous morning for a run."

"You should have let me know you were going out. I would have joined you."

Running was something Victoria had never been keen on. She found it monotonous. Her exercise program involved a very expensive trainer and the comfort of a home gym. She claimed that when it came to working out, she needed someone to push her.

"I wasn't sure how late you were up with Drew and didn't want to disturb you."

"Mrs. Farnes said you intended to run five miles. Is that what you normally do?"

"I fluctuate between two and seven depending on how much time I have."

"How long have you been running?"

She began unbuckling Drew from the stroller. The little boy reached for her, indicating he wanted to be picked up. "All my life. The only way I got any time by myself was if I put on my running shoes and hit the road."

"So if I offer to keep you company tomorrow, you'll turn me down?"

She shook her head. "I'd love to have you come along." She lifted Drew high in the air and spun him around. As his laughter filled the spacious foyer, she snuggled him against her chest and dropped a kiss on his head. "Have you had breakfast?"

Blake was so captivated by the mother/son moment that her question didn't initially register. After a pause, he said, "No. I was waiting until you got back."

"Then let's go eat. I'm starving."

She carried Drew into the kitchen and put him in the high chair Mrs. Farnes had set up at the table in the break-fast nook. While Blake fastened on Drew's bib, Bella helped the housekeeper carry over plates of eggs, bacon, pancakes, toast and fruit. Blake cut up a variety of things he knew Drew liked and placed them before his son.

"What are your plans for the day?" he asked, keeping one eye on Drew in case he decided the food wasn't to his liking and began to throw it.

"I thought I'd take Drew to the beach this morning. Maybe take him for a swim later this afternoon if it's warm enough."

"There's a car in the garage for you to use if you want to get out," Blake said. "There's the children's museum and a petting zoo at the Wilkinson Farm. With all the things to do in the area, I'm sure it will be easy to keep Drew entertained."

Bella gave him a wry smile. "At his age you can sit him in the kitchen with a pot and a wooden spoon to bang on it and he would be perfectly content."

Blake pictured the myriad of toys that crowded his son's room and realized what Bella said was completely true. Everything engaged Drew's imagination, from a brightly colored train that played songs when he pressed its buttons to a stainless-steel pot that made a racket when he banged on it.

"The beach sounds nice. Mind if I join you?"

Her smile was shy as she answered, "That would be nice."

"We can go out for lunch later."

"I'm sure Drew would like that." The phone strapped to her upper arm began to buzz. She unfastened the band and eyed the screen. "It's my brother. Excuse me for a second."

She got up from the table and strode out of the kitchen. Blake's gaze followed her departing form until Drew banged on his tray to get his father's attention.

"More banana?" Blake sliced the fruit for his son, then turned his attention to Bella's low voice.

"Another nine hundred?" she quizzed, her tone concerned. "But I already gave you five to buy the truck. What is the nine hundred for?" A long pause followed her question. "Is that the cheapest quote you got?" More silence. "I realize that the truck does you no good if it doesn't run. Okay. I'll see what I can do about the money." Her voice grew louder as she approached. "Elephant shoes," she said as she sat back down. With a sigh, she disconnected the call.

"That's a strange way to say goodbye."

She offered him a wan grin. "It's a family joke."

"Feel like telling me about it?" Blake buttered more toast and set it on her plate, then pushed the bowl of preserves her way.

"It started with my parents." Her mood perked up as she

began her tale. "They met through 4-H when they were teenagers, but lived in towns an hour apart so they didn't go to the same high school. But their schools competed against each other in football and basketball. My dad played both." Bella slathered preserves on her toast and cast a wry look Blake's way. "Naturally, my mom was a cheerleader so she was always rooting against my dad."

Blake had little trouble picturing the atmosphere in the small-town gymnasium where rivalries were fierce between the various communities. "Nothing like a little competition to keep things interesting."

"And apparently things were very interesting. My parents' senior year, Dad and some of his teammates crashed my mom's homecoming dance. I guess things got a little out of hand and my dad ended up getting his nose broken by his best friend when Dad stepped in to protect my mom from being hassled."

"And the rest is history?"

Bella shook her head. "Not even close. It became a Romeo and Juliet story. The two high schools were always pretty contentious, but after the fight at the homecoming dance, things got even worse."

"So your parents were star-crossed lovers?"

"Something like that. Anyway, they had to keep their romance a secret, and when they met in public, instead of saying 'I love you,' they'd say 'elephant shoes.'"

Her wistful grin told him the story had great meaning for her, but the punch line eluded him. "Why elephant shoes?"

"Read my lips." She paused a beat. "Elephant shoes. See?"

Lost in the pleasure of watching her mouth form the words, he neglected to notice what she was trying to tell him. "Sorry, I missed it. Do it again."

She rolled her eyes, but complied. "Elephant shoes."

This time he paid attention and the message came through

loud and clear. "It looks like you're saying 'I love you,'" he said with a short laugh. "Very clever."

"My mother came up with it."

Drew banged his palms on the high-chair tray and made happy noises, adding to the cheery vibe surrounding the small table.

"I think he likes the story, as well," Blake said with a chuckle. He caught a glimpse of the clock. They'd lingered over breakfast for more than an hour. Once again Bella's stories made time vanish. How could she be so against having a family of her own when hers was such an integral part of her life?

Blake was pouring a third cup of coffee as Mrs. Farnes approached the table and began to clear the dishes.

Bella got to her feet. "Let me help."

"No, dear. You've got enough to keep you busy." She nodded to Drew, who was busy smashing scrambled eggs and banana into his hair.

"Oh, Drew." Bella ran for a washcloth. By the time she returned, Mrs. Farnes had swept the last bits of food from the tray. "Thanks for your help," she told the housekeeper. "It really does take a village." Bella caught one of Drew's chubby hands and began applying the wet cloth. "I can't imagine how my mother did it. Before I was old enough to help, she had to handle three children under the age of six all on her own."

"Sounds like you grew up fast," Blake said, amused at the faces his son made while Bella cleaned food from his hair.

While Mrs. Farnes kept an eye on him, Bella and Blake ran upstairs for some warmer clothes. Although the day was heating up, the breeze on the beach would be cool, and she didn't want Drew catching cold on her watch. Blake followed Bella and Drew outside, a blanket and some plastic beach toys in his arms.

Because his house sat on five acres of land, the stretch

of beach in front of his property didn't see a lot of traffic. Bella spread out the blanket on the soft white sand and sat Drew in the middle of it. Blake lay on his side, his position perfect to watch both Bella and Drew. The infant showed little interest in the beauty surrounding them, preferring to focus his attention on the sand. This meant they had to watch him like a hawk, because he was determined to fill his mouth with handfuls of sand.

"Last night," Blake began.

Bella thrust her hand up, forestalling him. "I did some thinking."

"As did I."

"Me first," she insisted, determined to lay her cards on the table. "I imagine the idea of trusting another woman with your heart is unnerving."

His eyebrows twitched upward at her opening salvo. "It's positively terrifying," he retorted dryly.

She plowed on, ignoring his sarcasm. "You have to know that every woman in your social circle is going to set her sights on you."

"I am quite a catch." He was playing with her, letting her lead the conversation instead of demanding she get to the point.

"Yes, you are." Bella paused, her gaze on the horizon, her thoughts elsewhere.

"Bella?" he prompted. "Were you done making your point?"

His question jolted her back on track. "Not quite." She pulled the shovel out of Drew's mouth and demonstrated how it could be used to dig in the sand. "You are also the most guarded person I've ever met. You have to be doubly so after your divorce."

Blake could tell she was winding up to deliver a knock-out punch and awaited the results with keen interest. What notions had she bandied about in that adorable brain of hers these last few hours? He couldn't decide if this was a preamble to goodbye or a lecture on the evils of sexually harassing someone in his employ.

"Let me see if I'm clear on what you're saying. Women want me, but I've been burned."

"Exactly." Her rain-washed blue eyes regarded him solemnly. "That's why you picked me."

Now they were getting somewhere. At her heart, Bella was a practical woman. She would need to reconcile how, after they'd been nothing but friends for the months she was carrying Drew, he could suddenly desire her. Blake cursed himself for moving too fast. She would be skeptical of any explanation he offered. And how could he get her to accept why his desire for her had struck him so powerfully when he didn't fully understand it himself?

"I'm not following," he said, playing for time. "Why do you think I picked you?"

"Because I'm safe."

Blake couldn't believe what he was hearing. Safe? She had to be kidding. "Is that how you see yourself?"

"I'm a kindergarten teacher from a tiny town in Iowa. You are a sophisticated, wealthy businessman from New York City. When it comes to experience, I'm no match for you."

And that was a huge part of her charm. He liked her authenticity. She was a woman of substance and depth. She intrigued his mind in addition to captivating his body.

Blake stared at her profile and fell into the memory of their lovemaking. Desire hummed pleasantly along his nerves, the sensation muted, but poised to sharpen with the least provocation. She might be right to be concerned.

"I can see where you might get that idea," he said. But where was she headed with her analysis? Was she treating him to a tongue-in-cheek jab at his forceful personality, or was she worried he'd be too physically demanding?

"Also, you know I have no interest in marrying you. So there's no pressure."

She had everything all figured out, didn't she?

"You have no interest in marrying me?" Blake's amusement dimmed. If anyone other than Bella had made that statement, he would write it off as a woman willing to say anything to keep a man from bolting. But this was Bella, determined to stay childless.

"You probably find that hard to believe." She gave him a smug look. "But it's true. Plus, you don't have to worry whether or not I'll fall for you because you already know I won't."

"Am I so undesirable?" She was certainly making him feel that way.

"You know you're not," she retorted, treating him to a scowl. "In fact, you're very charming and terribly handsome."

"Which explains why you're completely immune."

She sighed. "Even if I believed Cinderella stories can come true—which I don't—the fact of the matter is you and Drew are a package deal. At some point you're going to want to get remarried to someone who can be a mother to him. That's not me."

She'd certainly thought the whole thing through. Too bad for her, he'd done some comprehensive strategizing of his own.

"Where does that leave us?"

"I was thinking a casual summer romance. Something to bridge the gap between your divorce from Victoria and the next Mrs. Blake Ford."

Blake couldn't believe what he was hearing. "How casual, exactly?"

"Great sex. No strings."

She looked so pleased with herself that Blake wanted to shake her until the ridiculous idea tumbled out of her mind.

Great sex. No strings. What man wouldn't jump at the opportunity?

It was impossible. And insulting. Did she really think he could spend the next two months getting to know her, making love to her and then just let her go?

Blake pitched his voice to disguise his annoyance and asked, "If we were to begin a no-strings arrangement, have you considered how we might go about it?"

"Not really. But if we were to do consider one, it would have to remain a secret."

This was just getting better and better. "Are you embarrassed to be with me?"

"I'm only thinking of your reputation."

"Why don't you let me worry about my reputation."

He brushed her hair off her shoulder and grazed his thumb along the line of her neck, feeling her tremble beneath his touch. Her eyes widened as he tugged her off balance. She wasn't quick enough to save herself and ended up tumbling onto the blanket beside him.

"Blake," she muttered in obvious warning.

He cupped her head and drew her closer. His lips grazed hers and he smiled when he felt her kissing him back. "Are you asking me to stop?"

"Yes." Rattled and flushed though she was, her tone was firm.

After several quick heartbeats, he complied.

"I think it's time I took Drew back up to the house. He'll need a bath before lunch." She got quickly to her feet and picked up Drew. "Do you mind bringing the blanket and his toys?"

"Not at all," he said. "I'll be up shortly."

Eight

With her nerves all stirred up, Bella was breathless by the time she reached the house. The mirror in the hall between the kitchen and foyer reflected a wild-eyed woman with windblown hair and bright red cheeks.

Why was it every time he touched her she came apart? Only the fact that they were on a public beach kept her from surrendering to the sensual light shimmering in his eyes.

"Hello?" a voice called from the entry.

Bella's heart plummeted when she spied Blake's ex-wife. For her impromptu visit, Victoria had chosen to wear a pair of wide-legged white linen pants and a sheer white blouse over a lacy camisole. Her long blond hair was fastened into a messy knot atop her head with loose tendrils framing her face. She wore gold sandals with four-inch heels. The look was perfect for a party at the yacht club or demonstrating to your ex-husband how much he was missing.

"Hello, Victoria." Bella shifted Drew's weight higher on her hip. "I didn't realize you were in the Hamptons."

"I'm staying with Blake's sister." Victoria's perfect lips curved into a smug smile.

It took a second to register that Blake's ex-wife wasn't the least bit surprised to see her. "I heard Jeanne rented a house nearby."

"Just three houses down. We're neighbors. Isn't that nice?"

While Bella wondered why Blake had neglected to mention this, Victoria rattled on. "I tried calling him earlier, but got his voice mail, so I thought I'd pop over and invite him out for lunch."

"He's down at the beach."

"Looks like you all were." For an instant Victoria's perfectly arched eyebrows came together. "It didn't take you long after my divorce to break your promise."

"Blake needed my help." Bella glanced behind her, wondering where he was. She would appreciate him running interference with his ex. "And the reason I made the promise was no longer valid."

"I'm still Drew's mother. We're still a family." Except for her initial greeting, Victoria hadn't paid Drew a bit of attention. Her focus was all on Bella.

Bella bit down on the inside of her lip to keep from firing back at Victoria. No need for the model-turned-actress to know how much Blake had shared about the reasons for his divorce.

"Of course you are." Bella decided the safest thing to do was change the subject. "How have you been?"

"Just terrible," Victoria said, her tone turning tragic. "I miss Blake. I made such a mistake leaving him."

Bella was at a loss for what to say. Last night Blake had held her in his arms, made her come alive. Not once had he mentioned that he'd had dinner with Victoria or that she was staying with his stepsister.

"I'm sure you did what you felt was best at the time,"

Bella murmured, grateful that Drew was beginning to fuss so she didn't have to meet Victoria's gaze.

"I was afraid. Blake put so much pressure on me to be the perfect mother. He has all these expectations because of what happened with his own mother."

Curiosity aroused by Victoria's declaration, Bella pinched her lips together to contain the questions that flooded her mind. Blake's past was none of her business. But her silence acted to prod Victoria to more revelations.

"He never really recovered from her abandonment. He was only eight at the time. It's why he expected me to stay at home and spend every waking second with Drew. But that's not who I am. My career makes me happy."

"Victoria—" Bella began, only to have the woman interrupt her.

"You can talk to him. You can make him understand that a woman can do both. Have a career and be a mother."

"I really don't want to get involved in what's going on between you and Blake."

"Aren't you already involved?" Victoria's gaze grew laser sharp. "Look at you. Blake and I have been divorced scarcely a few months and you're already moved into his house and taking care of his son. You're just one happy little family, aren't you?"

"I'm Drew's nanny. That's it." Unbidden memories of previous night rose into her mind and Bella felt heat rush into her cheeks.

Victoria's lips thinned. "You've wanted him all along, haven't you?"

"That's not true."

"Sure it is. I knew from the moment Blake introduced us that you would fall for him. A naive little farm girl from Iowa. What a laugh. I should have argued harder for a different surrogate."

Bella's breath caught in her throat. Victoria was a better

actress than any of them gave her credit for. Bella had had no idea Blake's ex-wife disliked her so much.

"I don't think we should be talking about this in front of Drew," she told Victoria.

The stunning former fashion model regarded her in disgust. "He's nine months old."

"He might not understand the words, but he's sensitive to tone and body language."

"Fine." Victoria leaned toward Bella and lowered her voice. "Since you're so worried about Drew, you'll want to make sure I only have to say this once. Keep your little crush on Blake to yourself. He and I are meant to be together. That's the way it is."

That she made no mention of Drew irritated Bella. "They're a package deal," she reminded the other woman. "Blake is devoted to his son. He's going to expect the woman he marries to be equally committed to Drew."

"And I suppose you think that's you?"

Bella was stunned by Victoria's vehemence. How was it possible that such a beautiful, successful woman could be intimidated by her? "I have no interest in marrying Blake."

"Why not? It would set you up for life. All your family's financial problems would be a thing of the past."

The slap of Victoria's words loosened Bella's tongue. "Like you, I don't want to be a mother."

"Yet here you are playing one to Drew."

"I'm his nanny," Bella repeated, enunciating each word so her message was clear. "Blake needed someone to fill in for a couple months. I needed money for my sister. It's nothing more than that."

"Then make sure it stays that way, because if anything you do keeps me from getting him back, I'll make sure he knows the truth about Drew."

Instinctively Bella clutched Drew tighter. Her heart jerked in alarm. "That will only hurt your relationship with Blake."

"Remember the mother who abandoned him? If he finds out you've done the same thing to your son, he will hate you forever."

Bella flinched away from the malice in Victoria's eyes. "My relationship with Blake is strictly professional. I'm his son's nanny," she reiterated. "If he doesn't want to reunite with you, it will not be because of anything I've said or done." Shaken by her encounter with Victoria, Bella headed for the stairs. "If you're looking for Blake, try the beach."

Without another word Victoria marched off, leaving Bella to ascend the stairs on shaky legs. Thanks to their little chat, Bella was no longer certain a summer fling with Blake was a good idea. As tempting as it was to spend the next couple of months *getting him out her system,* as Deidre had termed it, with Victoria back in the picture and angling for a reunion, Bella was better off returning her relationship with Blake to a professional footing.

While she ran Drew's bathwater, Bella stripped him out of his sandy attire. Either he was still energized by his time on the beach or Victoria's hostility had riled him up; whichever was the case, Bella had a heck of a time keeping the sand from scattering all over the bathroom. Once he was seated in the water, splashing happily, she sat down against the wall and wiped her forehead with the back of her hand, following Drew's antics with only half her attention.

It was peaceful sitting here. How many times had she watched her brothers or sisters in the tub? Too many to count.

Bella plucked Drew from the water and wrapped him in a thick towel. Cuddling him against her, she turned toward the door and spied Blake. How long had he been standing there? He'd showered but hadn't taken time to dry his hair. It had a tendency to curl when it was wet. The sight struck her as adorable, a ridiculous term to use for someone as vigorous and masculine as Blake.

"I'm sorry Drew's bath took so long." She stumbled over

her apology, thrown off balance by his clean scent and penetrating regard. "Give me a second to get him dressed for your lunch with Victoria. Is she still here or are you picking her up?"

"Neither."

He continued to loom in the doorway, barring her way. Butterflies swirled in her midsection at the way he overpowered the generous space with his strong personality and commanding form.

"But I thought…?"

Blake hooked his free hand around her neck and drew her close. Bella was too startled to avoid the lips that came down to claim hers. Hard and demanding, the kiss stole her breath. She had no choice but to yield to the hunger that surged through her. He devoured her in slow, deliberate strokes of his tongue and lips.

She murmured in protest as he eased back, but the sound of Drew's babbling reached through the fog of passion that held her enthralled. She twisted away from his kiss.

"Blake." Her fingers clutched Drew's towel. "You have to stop doing that."

"I like doing that." His voice was flat and emotionless. "I think you do, too."

She refused to respond to the challenge in his eyes. "We can't." She took a hurried step back when she realized her close proximity might be misconstrued as further invitation.

"You were singing a different tune half an hour ago." He kept his hands to himself, but his hot gaze was just as devastating to her willpower.

"I haven't been thinking straight for the past twenty-four hours." Seeing that he wasn't buying her explanation, Bella hurried on. "You have no idea how charming you can be."

"I know exactly how charming I can be, but you can't seriously expect me to believe that's why you slept with me."

"I'm attracted to you." Bella gave him a one-shoulder

shrug, but wouldn't meet his eyes. "I won't deny I wanted you. But after some more soul-searching, I realized the two of us engaging in a casual romp is just ridiculous."

"And naturally this has nothing to do with Victoria showing up here today? What did she say to you?"

"She wants you back." The breath Bella gathered was less steady than she would have wanted. "You, her and Drew are a family. I think you owe it to yourself to give it another try with her."

"The three of us are not a family. She left us." The way his own mother had left him.

Bella winced. Convincing Blake he was better off with his ex-wife wasn't going to be easy. "And she regrets that."

"Is that what she told you?"

"Yes."

"What else did she say?"

Here's where she had not wanted to go. "I told Victoria—and I'm going to tell you—I don't want to be involved in whatever's going on between you two."

"There's nothing going on."

"I don't think your ex-wife sees it that way."

"I don't care which way she sees it. The reality is she's not willing to give up her career to be a mother to Drew."

"Does she have to? Can't she do both?"

Victoria had been right about Blake's expectations. He wanted his wife to surrender everything she was in order to be Drew's mother. It was one thing if a woman wanted to put her family first, the way that Bella's mother had. It was something else for a man to insist that she do it.

"Her career isn't something that Vicky can do halfway. With her last play, I was lucky if she was home before ten at night. And that was before the play opened. She spent at most an hour or two with Drew a week."

"I would have made a rotten marriage counselor," Bella grumbled, beginning to see Blake's point. Both he and Victoria had valid issues. Irreconcilable differences had caused their marriage to end. "Maybe you two can find a way to compromise. Figure out some middle ground."

"She came by today to tell me she has an audition for a television series in Los Angeles. How are we supposed to be a family if we're on two different coasts?"

"She invited you to lunch. Why not go and hear her out?"

"Because I already have a date with you."

At the word *date* a sensation lanced along Bella's nerve endings. Excitement? Anxiety? Her emotions were too scrambled for her to distinguish one from the other. The last thing she needed right now was to be seen in public lunching with Blake. How was she supposed to keep Victoria from getting the wrong idea once the gossip began to spread?

"I know I agreed earlier to have lunch with you and Drew, but maybe it's not such a good idea for us to be seen together like that? People might get the wrong impression."

"People in general?" he echoed. "Or someone in particular?"

She had no intention of answering him. "Won't it look odd for you to be seen lunching with the help?"

His mouth twisted with displeasure. "Is it really my reputation you're worried about, or is it yours?"

"Mine." The instant the admission left her lips, she wished it back. "You probably think it's dumb that I value my privacy, but after growing up in a small town where everyone knew your business and having to share a house with seven nosy siblings, I've discovered that being anonymous is one of my favorite things about living in New York City."

Blake regarded her for a long, silent moment before nodding. "Fine. We'll drive up the coast to a little out-of-the-way place I know. The food is terrific and you won't have to worry about anyone spotting you with me. Happy?" He sounded anything but.

"Delirious." She gave the word the same sarcastic spin

he'd used, but her insides were dancing with joy. "Give me ten minutes to shower and get dressed."

"Take twenty. I'll dress Drew and meet you downstairs."

The second half of June vanished before Blake could tear himself away from East Hampton and return to New York City. He, Drew and Bella had settled into a nice routine.

They ran five miles before breakfast, ate eggs or pancakes, then Bella and Drew went to the beach while Blake worked in his office. They reconnected for lunch and while Drew napped, Blake discovered all sorts of new and interesting ways to make Bella moan. She had a delightful range of impassioned sounds and he was happy cataloging each one.

Once Drew woke, he and Bella would go for a swim and then play until dinner while Blake made calls to New York. They almost never went out. The beach house had become a cozy world for just the three of them. Leaving it would mean confronting reality. And Blake was certain neither he nor Bella wanted to do that.

He suspected his friends were wondering if he'd ever stop turning down invitations. He had little trouble imagining the gossip being exchanged over drinks at the club or shopping in town. His divorce from Vicky had been fast and quiet. He'd kept the reasons for it private, but something as juicy as Victoria Ford having an affair with Gregory Marshall wasn't something that could remain undiscovered.

His relationship with Bella was too new, too tenuous to survive the curiosity of his social circle. Nor was he ready to share her with anyone. He was enjoying having her to himself far too much.

After a long day at the office, he was glad to head home. The penthouse was a hollow shell without Drew, and he realized how easy it had been to forget his ordinary life in Manhattan and live a fantasy in East Hampton with his son and a woman who was a nurturing caretaker and an outstanding mistress.

Blake stood in the living room, a scotch in his hand, and contemplated Central Park. In another year Drew would be running over the grass with Blake in hot pursuit. He could almost hear his son's joyful giggles. And the woman who stood by and watched? Bella.

His breath caught. She'd been appearing more and more in his thoughts about the future. He'd pictured quiet dinners with her in the penthouse. Them pushing a stroller around the zoo. Attending Drew's soccer matches together. It was a very different life than he'd had with Vicky.

"Mr. Ford." Blake's housekeeper stood in the arch between the living room and front hallway.

He glanced at his watch. "Is it time for dinner already?"

"No." She advanced. "I was cleaning out the closet in the third bedroom. Mrs. Ford came by earlier this week and wanted to pick up some things she'd left behind." Mrs. Gordon paused and looked uncomfortable. "I told her I couldn't let her in without your say-so, but that I would pack everything up and get it delivered to her."

"That's fine." Blake was about to turn back to contemplating the view when he noticed an envelope in Mrs. Gordon's hand. "Is there something else?"

"This." She advanced toward him. "It fell out of a box filled with her old tax records."

Vicky had always handled her own money. Early in her career, a friend of hers had lost everything when her business manager embezzled from her. Blake had always enjoyed watching his wife sit at her desk and work her financial data. As frustrated as he often became with her frivolous nature, this was one aspect of her personality that he wholeheartedly appreciated.

"What is it?" Blake quizzed, taking the envelope from

his housekeeper. It had already been slit open, allowing him to remove the contents.

"It's a bill from the fertility clinic." Mrs. Marshall sounded worried.

Blake scanned the statement. It was indeed a bill. One that had only his wife's name on it. The bottom line was a great deal less than what they'd been told to expect for in vitro fertilization.

Probably because the services rendered had been for artificial insemination instead.

As the import of what he was reading sunk in, Blake felt his stomach drop. Thoughts spinning, he double-checked. Yes, Bella was listed as the patient. But she hadn't been implanted with fertilized eggs. She'd been impregnated with his sperm.

Drew wasn't Vicky's son.

He was Bella's.

With Blake in the city for a few days, Bella decided to take Drew on a tour of some local museums. East Hampton had a rich history that fascinated her. Established in 1648, it was one of America's earliest settlements. Fishing and farming was the way most made their living until the early part of the twentieth century, when the town began attracting the wealthy as well as artists and writers.

She started at Mulford Farm. Built around 1680, the house was remarkable in that it remained unchanged since 1750. In addition to being architecturally interesting, the fact that the Mulford family had owned the house for most of its existence offered insight into how they used the land and the buildings.

While Bella explored the rooms furnished with period pieces, Drew fell asleep in his stroller. He was exhausted after a difficult night of teething. Bella sympathized. She too was worn out, but her scholarly interest was stimulated by the house and the barn. She took a lot of pictures, knowing her father would find the layout of the barn intriguing.

Her phone rang as she was buckling Drew into his car seat. Thinking it was Blake, she answered.

"Hiya, sis." It was her sister Laney. At thirteen, she was the most social of all Bella's siblings.

Laney had two close friends who lived in town and when the three girls weren't together, they were texting or chatting through social media. To save her parents the cost of an additional line, Bella had put Laney on her cell plan. Plus, it offered her an opportunity to see how much time her sister spent "connecting."

"What's up?"

"I don't know if I told you that our choir got invited to Chicago to perform in August."

"That's fantastic."

"Mom and Dad aren't going to be able to chaperone and I was wondering if you could."

Bella sighed at her sister's request. It was something she'd done in the past. Laney had been in the choir since she turned nine. They'd often traveled to sing, but never to a city as big or as far away as Chicago.

"When is it?"

"August first through the sixth. We've raised almost all the money we need, but we're short two chaperones."

The timing of the trip wasn't great. Bella didn't know when Talia would be back and she didn't want to leave Blake in the lurch for that long. "I'm not sure I'm going to be able to do that."

"Come on, Bella, you've done it for me before." Which was why Laney expected her sister to drop everything and do it again. "We might not be able to go if we don't have enough chaperones."

The despair in Laney's voice was real and Bella winced.

She hated disappointing her sister, but she had an obligation to Blake, as well.

"I'm not saying no because I don't want to," she explained, ignoring the way Laney's request had caused a dip in her mood. "It's just that I have a job this summer and I'm not sure I can get away."

"Can't you ask them? Tell them how important it is. I'm sure they'll understand."

"This is important, too." Bella cursed her rising temper.

She didn't want to be cross with her sister. Laney was thirteen and excited about going to Chicago. Bella didn't blame her. If she'd had an opportunity to spend a few days there when she was her sister's age, she would have been over the moon.

"Please. Please. Please."

With each pleading syllable, Bella felt herself weakening. "I'll have to check and see if I can have the time off. I'll let you know later in the week."

"I need to know tomorrow. That's when they're deciding if they need to cancel the trip or not."

Behind Laney, Bella heard her mother's voice. A second later, Laney was replaced by her mother.

"Bella, we have everything in hand here. You don't need to ask your boss for time off."

As much as it would relieve Bella to believe that, she'd grown up hearing her mother utter the exact same phrase when things weren't the slightest bit under control.

"That's not the way it sounded."

"Your sister cannot expect you to fly to home so you can chaperone."

The weariness beneath her mother's exasperation tugged at Bella. She should be home helping out instead of living the good life in New York. It had been selfish of her to move so far away.

"I'm sure it will be okay with Blake," she assured her mother.

"Blake Ford? That nice man who called us a few weeks ago?"

Bella rolled her eyes at her mother's description of Blake. Many words could be used to describe the attractive CEO. *Nice* was probably not top on the list. Forceful. Determined. Persuasive. Sexy as hell. *Nice* was too tame.

"I'm working as his son's nanny for a couple months while his regular nanny recovers from a broken leg."

"It's wonderful that you can help him out. Don't you worry about Laney. Someone will step forward and be their chaperone."

Even though Bella had been relieved of responsibility, her sense of obligation lingered. "If no one does, give me a call back. I'm sure I can figure something out."

"Of course."

But Bella knew her mother wouldn't call. She never asked for help. She just tried to get it all done on her own. Only she never did. There was always something left undone. Pieces to be picked up by Bella. And now her other siblings. But were they helping out?

"How are things going there, Mom?"

"Terrific."

Bella wasn't sure why she asked. Her mother never showed any signs of stress. But it was always there, just below the unruffled surface. When Bella had lived on the farm, it had been easy to pitch in. These days, Bella worried all the time about what was going on, but she was too far away to help.

Except with money.

It was how she assuaged her guilt over living so far away. Sending money let her feel as if she was still able to make things easier on her parents.

"I'm glad to hear things are good."

"Oh dear, Laney has another call coming in. We'll talk soon. Elephant shoes."

And as Bella was echoing her mother's *I love you,* the phone went dead.

She slid behind the wheel, her enthusiasm for the outing fading fast. The familiar burden of responsibility had descended on her shoulders. Her mind told her to shake it off, but a lifetime of habit kept the weight right where it was.

Nine

The empty stretch of road before them taxed Blake's driving skills very little and gave him lots of time to brood. Beside him, Bella watched the landscape race past, as lost in her thoughts as he was. The only sound in the car was the musical toy attached to Drew's car seat. The tinny nursery rhymes kept the atmosphere from becoming completely awkward.

Three days had passed since he'd learned that Drew was Bella's biological child. Three days for him to run a gamut of emotions from shock to anger to deep sadness. When he'd thought she was only Drew's surrogate, he'd been dismayed that she'd decided that she didn't want any contact after Drew was born. The realization that she'd given up her own flesh and blood troubled him to the point where he had difficulty speaking to her.

How could Bella give up her child?

The question pounded him over and over.

So why hadn't he asked her?

Because he was afraid her explanation would answer an

even older question. How could Blake's mother have abandoned him? Deep down he'd never truly accepted that his mother was too miserable with his father to stay married to him. If she had to move back to France, couldn't Blake have spent some time with her? Summers? Holidays?

As a child it had been too painful to accept that she'd never really loved him. He'd made excuses that continued to be plausible today. His father was a controlling bastard who'd probably paid her well to disappear out of his son's life. But could a woman who loved her child be bought off?

Blake's grip tightened on the steering wheel as he thought about the thirty thousand dollars he'd paid Bella to be Drew's surrogate. She'd had no problems taking the money in exchange for her son.

"Tell me more about the vineyard we're going to," Bella prompted, breaking the heavy silence. Blake had arrived back at the beach house just that morning and announced they would be visiting some friends. "How do you know the owner?"

"He and I went to college together. We were both business majors, but even back then he had a passion for wine. His father expected him to take over the family business. They haven't spoken in five years."

"Because he bought the winery?" Bella shook her head in dismay. "What sort of parent cuts ties with their child because they don't do exactly what the parent expects?"

Incredulous, Blake glanced her way. "There are all kinds of reasons why parents turn their backs on their children." He hadn't meant to start this particular conversation with Bella when they were on their way to visit his friends, but he couldn't let the topic go without commenting.

"Is that a shot at Victoria or at me?"

Thanks to this week's revelations, Blake now understood that Vicky didn't care if she was in Drew's life. He was far more interested in why Bella had turned her back on him.

"Why did you walk away last fall?"

"Because he didn't need me. He had you and Victoria."

Her practical answer didn't make him feel any better. "And now that Victoria and I are divorced?" Blake knew it was too early to push his agenda, but he was too irritated to be patient. "Have you changed your mind about being a part of his life?"

"Don't you think that will confuse him when he's old enough to understand how he was conceived?"

More excuses. Blake unclenched his teeth and relaxed his jaw. "I think he'll be more confused when he finds out there's a woman who carried him for nine months who isn't in his life."

"And what happens when you remarry?" Her tone took on an aggressive note. "Do you really think your new wife will appreciate me hanging around when she's trying to develop a relationship with him?"

"That's a poor excuse."

"It's not. It's what happened." Bella must have heard the slip because she rushed on. "What will happen. If it was me, I wouldn't want another woman hanging around. Interfering."

The explanation Bella gave didn't sound like her rationale.

"Vicky asked you to stay away." Suddenly it all made sense. "That's why you took yourself out of the picture after Drew was born."

"She was terribly insecure about becoming a mother. If she'd been able to carry Drew, she wouldn't have felt so disengaged from the process."

"There's nothing wrong with Vicky that would keep her from getting pregnant," Blake said, curious how much his ex-wife had told Bella. "She was afraid of the damage a pregnancy would do to her body."

"But—" Bella sputtered to a stop. When Blake looked

over, she was staring at him in horror. "How do you know that?"

"A year ago, I found out she lied to me about her infertility."

Blake remembered finding his wife's birth control pills. He'd been too focused on starting a family to see that his wife wasn't ready—wasn't interested—in having children. And instead of being honest with him, she'd lied and gone along with his desire for a family. In the end, she'd chosen her career over him.

But now that she'd discovered that becoming an actress was tougher than she'd thought, she wanted him back. Did she really think him such a fool? Nothing about her had changed. When the next opportunity presented itself, she would leave them once more.

Bella stared at him in shock. "Is that why you are so resistant to reconciling?"

"It's part of the reason. A marriage based on lies doesn't have much hope of lasting, wouldn't you agree?"

"Absolutely." She knitted her fingers together in her lap. "I don't understand why she would do something like that."

"Maybe at first she hoped I'd eventually give up my desire to become a father and then we could continue our active social schedule. She'd gotten her first taste of acting and wanted to do more. That would be impossible if she was pregnant."

Blake had thought he'd gotten past his bitterness, but it rose in his gut like acid. "Perhaps you can understand now why I'm going to put Drew's needs first the next time I marry."

"I do. But Victoria is pretty determined to win you back."

"I agree. And it's even more complicated because my stepsister is encouraging her." Blake took his gaze off the road long enough to gauge Bella's readiness for his next words. She had no idea what was coming. "But I know when they see you and me together, both Jeanne and Vicky will realize I've determined to go forward with my life."

"Me?" Her voice cracked with skepticism. "I'm sure there are dozens of women that would be a better choice."

"Not better for Drew." Blake decided it was time for the gloves to come off. "I've thought about you a lot these last nine months."

"You thought about me?"

"I had a hard time with your refusal to be in Drew's life."

Bella's lips parted. She appeared to be grappling with what to say. Blake waited her out, wondering if she was ready to give him a different explanation than she had nine months ago.

At last she said, "I did it because Victoria asked me to."

That was a relief. It meant she wasn't the coldhearted woman she'd led him to believe.

"I understand and appreciate what you tried to do, however misguided." Blake took one of her hands in his and played with her fingers. "And that means there's nothing standing in the way of you being in Drew's life." *Or in mine.*

Bella pulled her hand free and stared out the side window. "In his life as what, exactly?" Her low voice was almost impossible to hear over the music coming from the backseat.

It was too early for Blake to reveal his true intentions. "As his mother."

Her huge sigh told him she'd been expecting his words. "But I'm not his mother."

"You gave him life."

"As part of a business arrangement."

Her answer kicked him hard in the gut. He ignored the ache and kept all pain from his voice. "Don't tell me that's all it was."

"What do you want me to say?" Heartache thrummed in her tone.

"All I want from you is the truth."

"Then here it is. If I'd had any hint how hard it would be to give him up, I would never have agreed to be your surrogate." She gathered a shaky breath. "Never in a million years would I have guessed how attached I would get to the child I was carrying."

Accepting her explanation gave him some peace. "You gave no indication that you felt that way while you were pregnant."

Her lips drooped at the corners. "I was supposed to be carrying a child that could never be mine. How would you have felt if I'd told you I never wanted to let Drew go?"

"Devastated."

She gave a tight nod. "Every day that went by I fell more deeply in love," Bella continued. "By the time I was in my final trimester, I was seriously considering breaking our contract and going back to Iowa with Drew."

Blake's pulse hitched at how close he'd come to losing his son. "What stopped you?"

"I thought I was ready to do anything to keep him until I came here and spent those two weeks with you…and Victoria. I couldn't put my happiness above yours."

He sensed she hadn't included Vicky in her deliberations. "Thank you. The gift you've given me is something I can never repay."

"You're welcome." A ghost of a smile flitted across her lips. "But you're wrong. The money you paid me saved my parents' farm."

"You never told me what you did with the money."

Her eyes glittered. "And from your tone, I gather you thought I blew it on stupid things like clothes and partying?"

"New York can be an expensive place to live and you did give me the impression you'd been sucked in by the glamour."

"I've always valued my privacy. When you live with nine other people, it's a rare commodity."

"So your parents kept their farm and I have a wonderful son." His anger at her deception about being Drew's biological mother was tempered by yet another example of her generous nature. "How exactly did *you* benefit from our arrangement?"

Her eyes widened at his question, as if she'd never thought to include herself in the equation. "I guess what I got out of it was a wonderful new life in New York City. I never would have stayed here if we hadn't met. The couple I originally came out here to meet chose a different surrogate and I was on the verge of returning to Iowa when I got a call from the clinic about you and Victoria needing a surrogate."

She appeared perfectly happy with how things had turned out, but Blake couldn't help but believe she deserved more.

"I think you are the most unselfish person I've ever met."

"I'm not as altruistic as you believe."

"Really?" He recalled the bits he'd overheard from her phone conversations over the last several weeks. "What did you do with the salary advance I gave you?"

"I gave it to my sister Kate for her semester studying abroad in Kenya."

"And the money you gave to Sean?"

"Repairs to the truck he just bought."

"A truck you helped him buy?"

"He got a job in town this summer. If he doesn't have a car, he won't be able to get to work. He's planning on going to college after high school. He'll need to save as much as possible. If I can help in this small way, it will make things a little easier on him."

"Does everyone in your family turn to you for financial help?"

"My parents do the best they can. Mom promised Sean six hundred dollars toward a truck, but then the tractor needed repairs." Bella looked resigned. "There's always something that needs fixing on the farm."

"I was wrong earlier," Blake said, amazed how she downplayed the number of sacrifices she made on behalf of her siblings. "You're a saint."

She laughed. "Hardly."

It seemed as if her family didn't hesitate to ask for all sorts of help. He considered how easy it would be for people to take advantage of her generous nature. Obviously Vicky had. He was beginning to understand why she'd be so reluctant to take on more responsibility with a family of her own.

"So who takes care of you?"

Her brows came together at his question. "I guess I do."

Blake picked up her hand and carried it to his lips. Kissing her reverently, he declared, "You deserve someone who is willing to put you first."

"I wouldn't know what that's like," she admitted, tugging to free herself. "I'm compulsively drawn to people who need my help. It's a pattern I've had no luck breaking. All my life I've taken care of my brothers and sisters. I don't know how to do anything else."

"That changes now." Blake saw the sign for the Rosewood Winery and braked. "From this moment forward, I'm going to satisfy your every whim. It's time you see what you've been missing."

While the car rolled along a long driveway lined with neat rows of grapes that stretched endlessly in either direction, Blake's promise reverberated in Bella's mind. He was going to satisfy her every whim? Did he have any idea how incredibly tempted she was to let him do just that?

What would it be like to have Blake spoil her rotten? Just being with him brought her a joy she'd never known before. At the deepest level, his strength lulled her anxieties. Bella knew that if she stopped pushing him away, he would make her deliriously happy. But for how long? What he wanted for himself and for Drew was someone who would be completely dedicated to being a wife and a mother.

Long ago Bella had promised herself if she ever married it would be to someone who didn't want to be tied down with kids. She wanted the freedom to travel, to be spontaneous, to not constantly worry about money. To put herself first.

The way Blake's ex-wife had.

There were many things to criticize about Victoria's behavior, but sometimes Bella envied the ex-model's capacity for guilt-free self-indulgence. It would be nice to keep the money Blake was paying her instead of doling it out to her siblings. At the rate things were going back home, would her nest egg still be intact when it came time for the winter trip to the Caribbean?

"I need to warn you," Blake said as he stopped the car in front of a house straight out of the Tuscan countryside. "If Sam starts talking about making wine, he will not stop unless you tell him to. I think I mentioned that he's been obsessed with wine as long as I've known him. The same thing goes for growing grapes."

"But we're here to visit his winery." Bella stepped out of the car and stretched. The drive had taken a little less than an hour, but their conversation hadn't been an easy one and all her tension had sunk deep in her muscles. "Won't he expect us to be interested in it?"

Before Blake could answer, the front door opened and a woman appeared. While Bella unfastened Drew's car seat, the leggy redhead threw her arms around Blake.

"How wonderful to see you," she cried. "And you brought Drew."

"Julie, this is Bella."

"What a pleasure to meet you," Julie said.

Bella couldn't help but like the woman's energy. "Likewise."

"Where's Sam?" Blake asked as Julie coaxed a smile from a suddenly shy Drew.

"Do you really need to ask?" Julie hitched her head toward a group of buildings. "Why don't you go say hello and tell him lunch will be served in fifteen minutes. Bella, Drew and I will go get acquainted."

Julie led Bella around the house to a shady patio where several wicker chairs had been placed to take advantage of the views of the surrounding gardens and the acres of neatly planted grapes.

"I can't get over how beautiful it is," Bella exclaimed. "It looks just like the pictures I've seen of Italy. How big is your property?"

"About a hundred acres. Fifty-five of it is planted with grapes. The rest is pasture and my training facilities."

"Blake mentioned you train horses. How long have you been doing that?"

"Professionally for about five years, but I grew up competing in dressage and eventing. It was Sam's idea. I don't know if Blake mentioned to you how obsessed my husband is about his wine."

"He said Sam would talk my ear off if I let him."

Julie laughed. "That he will. Before he and I got married, I was worried how I was going to keep myself occupied. I don't share my husband's passion for grapes and fermenting. Sam suggested I open a training facility and then found us a vineyard with a large stable, riding ring and extensive paddocks. Our activities couldn't be more different, and yet somehow it feels as if we're working together."

"It sounds like a perfect arrangement."

Julie's blissful expression gave Bella a momentary pang. This was the sort of harmony her parents shared. Dad was in charge of the fields and the livestock. Mom looked after the heart and soul of the farm: her husband and her children. Together they kept the farm running and the family solid.

Resentment over her parents' decision to have so many children had kept Bella from recognizing how well they worked together. Sure, her brothers and sisters had complained about wearing hand-me-downs and having to share toys and electronic devices, but there was no question they'd all grown up in a loving household.

"I hope you don't mind my asking," Julie began. "But how is it you are spending the summer with Blake and Drew? I thought you told Blake you didn't want any contact with Drew."

The question caused Bella's stomach to wrench. Obviously Julie knew a great deal about Blake's business. Bella debated how to answer, then decided he wouldn't mind if she explained. "You probably think there's something wrong with me." She wouldn't blame Julie if she did. "I must be a horrible person to not want this amazing child in my life."

"*Horrible* is a little strong." Julie's hesitation made Bella like her all the more. "At first I assumed you were just in it for the money. But the way Blake had described you, that didn't make sense."

Curiosity got the better of her. "How did Blake describe me?"

"I believe he called you the perfect mother."

Bella felt the jolt clear to her toes. Her muscles quivered in the aftermath of the shock. "When did he say that?"

"Last summer. I've known Blake for a lot of years and I don't remember ever seeing him as happy as he was last year. When he and Victoria came to our five-year anniversary party last August, you and the baby were all he talked about."

"Oh, dear," Bella murmured beneath her breath.

Had Victoria overheard Blake's description? Was that what had prompted her to demand Bella stay away from Drew? If Blake was right and Victoria was feeling insecure about being a mother, that could explain why she acted as she had. "I think he was really stunned when you left. He thought you were planning to be a part of Drew's life."

"I did what I thought was best for all of them," Bella explained. "And to be honest, it was no easier for me." Feeling tears burn her eyes, Bella inhaled deeply, striving for calm. Those days following Drew's birth had been some of the darkest she'd ever known.

"I think I understand. It would have killed me to give up my daughter." Julie's quiet sympathy pulled Bella back from the edge. "And it looks like you're making up for it now. He obviously adores you."

Bella glanced down and realized Drew was staring up at her in that unnerving way he had. Their eyes met and he grinned. His expression was so adorable Bella couldn't help but smile back. She knew it was crazy to feel as if Drew recognized her as his mother. After all, she'd only been back in his life for a few weeks. But every time she thought about having to leave him again, a ball of agony settled in her chest.

"Here come the boys," Julie announced. "And my daughter, Lindsay. I can't believe Blake got Sam away from his tanks in time for lunch."

Blake and a tall blond man, carrying a four-year-old with copper ringlets, closed the distance to the patio with matching long strides. Setting down the little girl, Sam introduced himself to Bella with a bone-crushing handshake and tossed Drew in the air, making the boy scream with delight.

Since the weather was perfect, Julie insisted they eat outside. Halfway through the meal, Drew began to fuss and Bella went into the kitchen to heat up a bottle. By the time she returned, Blake had calmed the boy down and insisted on feeding him so Bella could finish her lunch.

Remembering what he'd said about satisfying her every whim, she couldn't help but appreciate his actions. Granted, Drew was his son, but she was the one getting paid to take care of him. Blake could have expected her to let her meal

go uneaten while he continued his uninterrupted. But tha
wasn't his parenting style.

Each night they traded off who got up when Drew begar
to cry. Heat crowded Bella's cheeks at the memory of wha
they were usually doing in the moments before the boy awak
ened. The easy intimacy between her and Blake continued tc
amaze her. Was it possible only weeks had passed since he'c
shown up at her school? Her level of familiarity with fathe
and son made it feel as if she'd been with them for months

Bella's phone buzzed, signaling she had a text. Thinking
it was Deidre or maybe her brother, she peeked at the screen.
The message leached the afternoon of all its pleasure.

Mrs. Farnes said you are having lunch with Blake. I warnec
you.

"Bella?" Julie's voice brought back the sunshine. "Are
you all right? You look as if you've gotten some bad news."

"No. I'm fine," she lied, smoothing her expression into a
half smile. "With a family as large as mine, there's always
drama."

"You have to tell me all about it," Julie insisted. "I'm an
only child and I've always wondered what it would be like
to have a big family."

Glad for the distraction, Bella began regaling Julie with
stories of her family in Iowa, while in the back of her mind
she replayed Victoria's message over and over. Would Blake's
ex-wife follow through on her threat?

Now that Bella realized having Drew in her life was as
necessary as breathing, would Blake find out the truth and
hate her for abandoning her son? He'd been so angry at her
decision when she'd only been Drew's surrogate. How betrayed would he feel if he knew that Bella was Drew's biological mother?

Of course, that bombshell would have devastating repercussions for Victoria, as well. Blake's ex-wife had to know that he would be unlikely to forgive her deception. But would she realize that in time to stop all their lives from being ruined?

Ten

Blake stood in the hallway outside his son's nursery and listened to Bella rambling in a soothing tone to Drew. Her words weren't exceptional, just a list of all the things they would do the following day if he would just settle down and go to sleep, but something about the quality of her voice captured his attention.

She sounded sad.

Who was to blame? Blake ran the day through his mind. Their conversation on the ride to the winery had been serious, but he'd stayed away from anything that would upset her. Bella had enjoyed meeting Julie and Sam. They'd all laughed a great deal at lunch as Bella regaled them with tales of her family.

She was a natural storyteller, blending drama and comedy to keep them completely engaged. Was this what she did for her students? No wonder they'd all given her such fierce hugs goodbye.

The day he'd stopped by her school, he'd sat in the car for

a long time watching her. For nine long months, she'd been on his mind. He'd gone through an entire emotional range after she'd walked out of Drew's life. When he'd found out the truth about Bella being Drew's biological mother, the elusive piece of the puzzle had fallen into place: he'd understood why Vicky had lacked any maternal instinct toward Drew. But until today, Bella's behavior had been less clear. The question that had plagued him all his life had one answer.

Why did a mother abandon her child?

In Bella's case it was because she'd sacrificed her own happiness to give Drew two parents who adored him. Or so she'd been led to believe.

"Elephant shoes."

Despite their being spoken softly, the words reached Blake's ear. His heart thumped hard. If he'd had any lingering doubts about Bella's true feelings for her son, they were completely eradicated. She loved Drew.

Blake entered the room and spoke softly. "How's he doing?"

"He's finally asleep." She smiled as Blake joined her at the crib. "It was touch and go for the last fifteen minutes, but I think exhaustion finally won out."

"That's fast work. Usually when he's fighting sleep it takes me an hour to get him down."

Her left shoulder rose and fell. "I've had a lot more practice with stubborn children than you have. My brother Scott was the worst. He used to stand in his crib and cry for hours. Ever try getting your homework done while a kid is screaming at the top of his lungs?"

"As an only child, I never had that problem."

Bella sighed. "It would have been wonderful to grow up an only child."

"It would have been nice to grow up with a houseful of siblings."

"I guess everyone wants what they don't have," Bella said.

"That's not always true." Blake slid his arms around her waist and pulled her snug against his body. "Some of us appreciate the things we do have."

When he bent to kiss her, her lips were parted and waiting. All his anger and doubts about this being the right thing for any of them vanished as he pulled her breath into his lungs and claimed her mouth. Her soft moan unleashed the fierce hunger he'd been holding back all day. She belonged in his arms. In his bed. He turned his back on logic and sent his palms gliding along her curves.

She rose onto her toes and tunneled her fingers into his hair. The hot, urgent dance of her tongue with his said that she'd missed him.

"Make love to me, Blake."

He needed no further urging. Sweeping her into his arms, he carried her from the nursery. His room was a few steps down the hall, but his impatience to have her naked beneath him made his bed seem a lot farther away. The mattress yielded beneath their combined weight. Bella sighed as he stripped off her shirt and set his mouth against her throat. Her fingers worked at his buttons, their progress unsteady. Then it was his turn to groan as she spread the edges of his shirt wide and coasted her palms along his skin. She skimmed the shirt off his shoulders and down his arms. He tossed the garment aside and bent to glide his tongue along the lacy border of her bra.

"You're beautiful," he murmured, grazing his teeth against her tight nipple.

She gasped. "Do that again."

He complied with a smile. Her hips moved restlessly as he teased her through the bra's thin fabric. Once again he was captivated by how responsive she was to his touch. He kissed his way down her flat stomach, the muscles quivering beneath his lips, to the waistband of her pants. Moving with deliberate intent, he unfastened the button and slid down the zipper. She raised her hips as he applied downward pressure to the material. In seconds she lay before him clad only in her underwear.

Blake paused to admire her delectable curves and long legs before stripping out of his pants and returning naked to slip between Bella's legs. With his erection sandwiched between them, Blake enjoyed the torment of her hands as she coasted her palms over his back and butt. He caught her hips and rolled them until he lay on his back with her on top of him.

Setting her palms on his shoulder, she pushed into a sitting position. For a long moment she stared down at him, her expression a study in wonder as she acclimatized herself to this new position. Then she trailed her fingers over his chest, taking a long moment to tease his nipples until they tightened in delight. Beneath her his erection jumped. She grinned.

"You like that," she said.

"I like everything you do to me."

"I haven't done much." She looked him over. "You pretty much take me by storm every time we make love."

"Tonight it can be lady's choice." He'd gladly surrender himself to her hands.

She hummed, considering. "Well, if that's the case..."

With a sly smile, she lowered her torso, placed her elbows on either side of his head and kissed him with rising passion. Her position offered Blake the perfect access to the most sensitive places on her body. Imitating what she'd done to him earlier, he eased his palms down her back, paying homage to each inch of silky skin and every bump of spine. Anticipation had rubbed him raw by the time he curved his fingers over the soft mounds of her backside. He stroked his fingertips along the seam between her buttocks and felt her shudder as he grazed down the heat between her thighs. She'd soaked through the fabric, as aroused as he by their foreplay. Her hips shifted in rhythm to his light touch while her breath rushed in and out of her lungs. She pushed back until she could glare down at him.

"This is supposed to be my turn," she reminded him, her voice unsteady.

"You can't seriously expect me to just lie here and take it." He watched her bite her lip as he slipped his finger beneath her underwear.

Reaching back, she seized his hands and pinned them to the mattress. "That's exactly what I expect."

"For how long?"

She considered the clock on his nightstand. "Half an hour?"

"Three minutes," he suggested, convinced that was all he could bear.

"Fifteen."

The urge to drive up inside her and feel her tight walls close around him would overtake him long before that. "Four."

His counteroffer wasn't to her liking. Her expression grew stern. "When negotiating you're supposed to meet the other party halfway."

"That's not how I made my millions."

"Ten."

"Five."

She nodded. "Five." And then she reached up and unfastened her bra. It flew across the room and before it landed, she'd settled her mouth over one of his nipples. The hot, wet tug shot a bolt of lust straight to his groin. Blake gathered two handfuls of sheet as a groan erupted from his throat.

In the end he lasted four and a half minutes, each second counted out as her exploration taxed his willpower. But she was having such a fine time trailing her lips over his chest, her fingertips over his legs that he endured the sweet torment until she seized his erection and nearly put an end to their interlude with one swift stroke.

"Time's up," he announced, catching her by the wrist. Before she could protest, he flipped her onto her back and pinned her beneath him. "It's my turn."

"That wasn't five minutes."

"Are you sure? Damn it, Bella."

She'd wrapped her thighs around his hips, bringing him into contact with her core. Only her panties kept them apart.

"Take these off." Fingers bit into his hand as she guided him to her underwear. "Or rip them off. I don't care. I need to feel you inside me."

"Your wish is my command."

But first he sheathed himself in protection. He knew how fast his willpower diminished once she was completely naked. By the time he turned back to Bella, she'd stripped herself bare and knelt behind him.

Her lips on his shoulder made him smile. Her eager fingers trailing up his thighs, however, shortened his breath. In a flash he'd snatched her into his arms and rolled them across the mattress. Once again, he stopped with her above him.

Without words, she understood what he wanted and positioned herself so that just the head of his erection penetrated her. Her lips curved in a blissful smile as she slowly lowered herself onto his shaft. By the time she'd fully encased him, Blake was certain he'd never seen a more beautiful sight.

The first hint of orgasm hit Bella before she'd taken in all of Blake's considerable length. Being on top offered her a whole new sensation. The bite of his fingers on her hips heightened the wildness rampaging through her. So did his expression of utter satisfaction.

As the first wave of pleasure hit her, she rotated her hips, experimenting with driving herself against his pelvic bone, and then had nothing more to do but hang on for dear life as he gently pumped into her. She bit her lip to hold back her cries, not wanting to disturb Drew. Maybe if they were very lucky, he would sleep through the night and Bella could linger in Blake's bed until dawn.

Suddenly she couldn't breathe. Her focus intensified on the bliss crashing through her body. It spun her in circles and catapulted her outward in a thousand different directions. Dimly she heard a raspy voice fill the room, but didn't realize it belonged to her until she returned to her body and spied Blake grinning at her.

"That was spectacular," he told her, reverence below the delight in his tone. "You are a firecracker."

With the heat of her orgasm blazing beneath her skin, Bella would never have believed she could feel hotter, but Blake's compliment turned her into an inferno.

She clapped her hands to her hot cheeks. "I've never been this way before. You bring it out of me."

Blake drew her palms to his lips and kissed each one, setting her body to tingling all over again. In turn, she grasped his hands and brought them to her breasts. He fondled her, tweaking her sensitized nipples and reawakening the desire momentarily sated by her climax. She rocked her hips. Inside her, Blake remained thick and hard. He hissed through his teeth as she began to move up and down on him.

"That's it," he told her, abandoning her breasts to show her exactly the way he wanted her to move.

She only had enough breath for one word. "Wow!"

As fast as she'd peaked before, this time the climb was slower. She had time to imprint Blake's scent. The salty taste of his skin. His low murmurs of encouragement. By the time he quickened his pace and began thrusting his way to his own completion, Bella knew she'd never escape the memory of this night.

Blake's movements grew more frantic. He was close. Bella felt the leading edge of another abyss, but she wasn't going to get there before Blake finished, until his fingers slid between their bodies.

"Come with me," he growled, touching her with the perfect pressure to make her explode. A second later he began to shudder with the power of his orgasm.

And then she was following him. Their cries were little more than low eruptions of satisfaction, but they crescendoed in harmony.

In the aftermath, Bella settled against his side, her cheek on his strong chest. With Blake's fingers drifting up and down her spine, she floated on a cloud of contentment. Telling him about her family this afternoon had torn down the last of the walls she'd erected to keep him at bay. She'd opened herself to him and the intimacy left her wanting to understand him better.

"Today you let me go on and on about growing up on the farm. I'd love to hear a little bit about your childhood."

Beneath her cheek, Blake's chest froze as if his breath had stopped. It was a long moment before he spoke. "Mostly it was lonely."

"Because your dad worked so much?"

"And because my mother spent more than half the year in Paris. Then she moved there permanently shortly after I turned eight."

He was so terse that Bella wondered if she should have left well enough alone. "Is that why you never talk about her?"

"There isn't much to talk about. She was beautiful and sang in French when she was happy. Often when I came home from school, she would be sitting by the window staring out at the park."

Bella's chest ached at the images of his childhood that his words conjured. No wonder he'd been so furious with her for deciding against staying in Drew's life. He didn't want his son to lack for a mother's love. Even a surrogate mom. "Do you ever speak with her?"

"Every birthday she sends me a card. It's the only contact we have."

"Is that a mutual decision?"

"When I was a kid, she never responded to any of my letters or answered when I called her. In time I gave up. After my dad died, she tried to get ahold of me, but I was old enough not to need her anymore."

Blake's blunt words and neutral tone wrenched at Bella, but there was more she had to know.

"Do you know why she left?"

"My father told me she missed her family in Paris. I imagine she thought he would make all her dreams come true when she married him, but he worked all the time and she was lonely."

"I'm sure that was very hard on you."

Another man with Blake's experience might never open himself up to love and marriage. It said a great deal about his strong, passionate heart that he'd let Victoria in. Bella could only hope the next woman he chose would be worthy of him.

"It took me a long time to accept that it wasn't my fault she left."

Bella ached for every day that Blake had carried the burden of his mother's abandonment. Often when Mommy or Daddy left, the remaining parent didn't explain to their children that adults could be selfish. She suspected Blake's father had been one of those.

"Now perhaps you understand why it was so important that you be in Drew's life."

"I've been doing a lot of thinking about that," she began, pushing up on her elbow so she could gaze into Blake's eyes. "I want to be in Drew's life. Our connection might be a bit unconventional, but I should be there for him whether or not he needs me."

Blake cupped her cheek and pulled her toward him for

a long, slow kiss. There was more gratitude than passion in the contact, but Bella was smiling when he released her.

His intense blue-gray eyes were soft with appreciation as he gazed at her. "Thank you."

"I should be the one to thank you. Drew is special. I'm so glad to be a part of his life."

"I intend for you to be part of my life, as well," Blake declared as he rolled her onto her back and blurred her thoughts with another heart-stopping kiss.

As he began making love to her all over again, Bella mulled his words and wondered what the future would hold once they returned to New York City and settled back into their separate lives. The freedom she'd craved grew less and less appealing with each day that passed, and it was becoming more and more clear that the obligations she hoped to avoid by not having a family were not easy to shake even if she wanted to.

And now she was caught in a dilemma of her own making. She was falling in love with the man who'd fathered the child she'd given up. The responsibilities she'd hoped to avoid were now what she longed to have. Marriage. Children. She wanted it all. And with the man who, if he ever discovered how she'd conspired with his wife to deceive him, would never be able to forgive her.

While the hallways and offices of his New York City investment company hummed industriously beyond his closed door, Blake sat in the stillness of his large corner office and eyed the selection of engagement rings the jeweler had brought for his inspection. There were probably a hundred carats of diamonds twinkling at him, each more beautiful than the last. The decision was easy. His eye had fallen on the ring immediately. It was simply a matter of indicating his choice.

The jeweler sat across the desk from him as if he had all

the time in the world. Blake appreciated the silence, because he wasn't just picking out a ring—he was making a decision that would affect the rest of his life.

Was marrying Bella the best idea? He'd been unable to answer the question in the ten days since they'd visited Sam and Julie, despite the increased intimacy he and Bella now shared. Talking about how she helped out her family and discussing his mother's abandonment had given him a deeper sense of connection with her.

But she'd kept from him that she—not Vicky—was Drew's biological mother. Could he trust that Bella wouldn't feel burdened by responsibility at any point in the future and change her mind about parenting her son? It was obvious that she loved Drew and he adored her, but was she ready to commit to being a family?

Should he let her remain as a part-time mom who saw Drew a few times a week? He'd rather she be fully in their lives, the full-time mother who got Drew up in the morning, took care of him all day and put him to bed at night. A mother who then became a wife. His wife. A wife he could worship with his body and cherish with his heart. But could that happen while he held on to his doubts?

Blake picked up the ring he'd chosen and gazed at it while the jeweler took care of the paperwork.

An enormous lie still lay between them.

After much deliberation, he'd decided not to confront her with his son's true biology. She must never believe he was marrying her because Drew was her biological child.

His first priority was his son's happiness. Drew deserved a mother who was willing to give him everything. He wanted Drew to have the sort of childhood Blake had been denied. To feel secure and loved. He should never need to question if there was something he'd done to cause his mother to leave.

Whatever it took to make his son happy, Blake would do. Any benefit he derived was a fortuitous byproduct. That he and Bella were good together was secondary to his son having a mother who loved him.

And while Bella was keeping Drew happy, Blake would make certain he took care of her. In every way possible.

A breeze off the Atlantic and the shade of a large umbrella kept Bella and Drew from feeling the worst of the afternoon sun. She'd still applied a liberal amount of sunscreen to his skin. Despite her sunglasses, she squinted against the glare coming off the pool's reflective surface. Humming along with the children's songs playing from speakers attached to the outside of the pool house, Bella carried Drew into the cool water.

The pool had been designed with a shallow shelf large enough to hold two lounge chairs. It was ideal for Drew because he could stand in the water. In the past two weeks, he'd become increasingly impatient with being held and when set down liked to pull himself up on the closest piece of furniture to him.

Bella had taken to walking with him on the lawn to strengthen his legs and improve his balance. Before long he would be walking on his own and she was determined to be around to witness his first steps.

Her phone began to ring as she was drying off Drew. It was Sean. She sighed, hoping he wasn't calling to borrow more money for repairs. She never should have lent him the money to buy the truck if she'd known he hadn't had their dad check it out first.

"You are the best sister ever," he exclaimed, barely giving her a chance to say hello.

"Thanks?" She wasn't sure what had brought on such enthusiastic accolades.

"It's absolutely the best."

"It's the best what?"

"Truck."

"I'm glad," she said, relieved that her savings account wasn't going to suffer any further withdrawals. "So nothing else has gone wrong with it?"

"How could anything go wrong with it?" He crowed. "It's brand-new."

Bella felt as if she and Sean were having two completely different conversations. "What's brand-new?"

"The truck."

"You mean it's *like* brand-new." Bella was developing a sinking feeling in her gut.

"No. I mean it *is* brand-new. The guy from the dealership delivered it an hour ago. He said I should thank my sister."

"Sean, I didn't buy you a new truck." But she had an idea who might have. "Let me call you back."

She hung up on her brother and scooped up Drew. As she marched up to the house, uneasy thoughts tumbled through her mind. There was only one way a brand-new truck could have been delivered to her brother.

Bella rushed into Blake's office. "Did you buy my brother a truck and say it came from me?"

"Yes."

Drew squirmed in her arms and she set him on the ground at her feet.

"Why would you do that?"

"Because you were giving him all your hard-earned money to repair the truck he had."

His matter-of-fact tone increased her exasperation. Bella glared at Blake, barely registering the chill of Drew's damp fingers against her bare legs as he pushed himself to his feet.

"It's too much. How am I supposed to repay you?"

"I don't expect you to."

Why was he helping her like this? She was an employee. He was paying her to watch his son.

But they were also sleeping together. And even though her heart wanted more, she'd never expected their relationship to be anything other than a casual summer fling. Now he was helping her in a huge way. What was she supposed to think?

Blake got up and came around his desk. His expression warned her that he intended to kiss away her concerns. She backed up two steps and lifted her hand to ward him off. His attention shifted to the space she'd just vacated.

"Look," Blake exclaimed, breaking into a broad grin.

Bella followed his gaze in time to see Drew toddle three steps to reach his father. Her annoyance vanished as Drew clutched his father's pant leg and gave a triumphant cry. His first steps and she'd been there to share the moment with Blake. At the same instant the momentous occasion registered, Blake's gaze shifted to her and she realized that he recognized the significance, as well.

"Marry me."

The proposal wasn't at all what she'd expected Blake to say. Her mouth dropped open, but she had no words. Blake scooped Drew into his arms, seeming not to notice that his son wore a wet bathing suit, and caught Bella about the waist.

"Marry me," he repeated, his eyes burning fiercely. "I want us to be a family."

This same longing had been growing in her ever since coming to the Hamptons, but Bella shook her head. "That's what I want, too—"

But before she could go on to explain the improbability of that happening, Blake gave her a kiss that was impulsive yet tender. Her body came to life as it always did when he touched her, but it was her heart that escaped the protective walls she'd built and soared free.

Blake loved her. The knowledge gave her the confidence she needed to trust her own heart. To accept that the right path for her was not to be free of responsibilities and obligations, but to embrace them the way Blake was embracing her. No wonder her mother had wanted a whole bunch of kids. They were a tangible reflection of her great love for Bella's father and for the life they had together.

As soon as Blake let her come up for air, she answered his proposal with all the joy in her. "Yes. Oh, yes." She set her head on Blake's shoulder and stared down at her son. "I want us to be a family."

Drew babbled at her, adding his own opinion to the mix.

Blake laughed. "I think we have a unanimous vote."

"It sounds that way." Bella rose on tiptoe and gave Blake a quick kiss. "And now I think we should get out of these wet clothes."

"While I love the way your mind works—" his hand slid downward from the small of her back, fingers trailing along the edge of her bikini bottoms "—I still have a couple calls to make before I'm free for the afternoon."

"That's not what I meant," she said, plucking Drew from his grasp. "We came straight from the pool…" Bella suddenly remembered why she'd charged up here in the first place. "You bought my brother a truck. Why?"

"I want to take care of you. Helping out your family is one way I can do that."

Relief made her knees wobble. She'd been the strong one for so long. "No one has ever taken care of me before."

"That's about to change. I don't ever want you to feel anxious or worried again."

The relief that washed through her was like a tsunami. It mowed down all her feelings of obligation, resentment and guilt and left behind a clean slate that she could use to build her new life upon.

"Thank you." The words were inadequate. She'd been transformed by his commitment to her. A tear escaped her eye. Not wanting to spoil the moment by losing control and sobbing in front of him, Bella dashed away the moisture with the back of her hand and set her cheek against the top of Drew's head. "I'd better get him changed."

Blake accompanied them upstairs and headed into his room for dry clothes. Bella carried Drew into her bathroom and stripped them both out of their swimming suits. She'd found that the easiest way to keep an eye on Drew and at the same time get them both cleaned up after visiting the beach or the pool was to bring him into the shower with her. There was plenty of space for Drew to sit at one end, out of the range of the spray, and play in the water while she rinsed off sand or chlorine.

Today, however, he'd discovered walking and used the wall for balance as he navigated from one end of the shower stall to the other. By the time she turned off the water and wrapped towels around them both, Drew was babbling happily at his newly acquired skills. It was then that Bella realized keeping track of him was going to be a full-time job.

The thought made her knees weak. She dropped to the bed and replayed the conversation she'd had with Victoria. Blake would expect Bella to give up her job at St. Vincent's and become a full-time mother. Drew squirmed on her lap, impatient at being held. She set him on the floor and quickly dressed. She braided her damp hair and chased after him into the hall. He was nowhere to be found and she raced to the open stairs, worried that he'd fallen down them.

Behind her came a wail and Bella spun around in relief. The sound had come from the nursery. And that's when it hit her that whether she was ready to accept it or not, in her heart, she was Drew's full-time mom and she would be miserable if she wasn't spending every waking minute taking care of him.

Eleven

Pushing Drew's stroller along Main Street in East Hampton was slow going. Bella had to stop frequently to avoid running over the people who were window-shopping along the thoroughfare. She was taking Drew for ice cream at a place she'd discovered the summer before. This was only her second trip into town. Drew was an active child. He preferred the beach and the pool to sitting in his stroller.

After purchasing a scoop of chocolate, Bella found a shady bench and sat down to share the treat with Drew. Where he'd been cranky the moment before, bored with his enforced immobility, the second the ice cream hit his taste buds, he was all delighted smiles and happy baby sounds.

She'd scraped the last of the chocolate from the cup and was steering the spoon toward Drew's open mouth when a woman's voice hailed them.

"Hello."

Bella looked up and saw Blake's stepsister sailing up the sidewalk toward them. Her attention was fixed on Drew, but she shot a friendly smile at Bella before joining her on the bench.

"You should have told me you were bringing Drew into town. We could have come shopping together." Jeanne set down her purchases. Half a dozen bags of various sizes pooled around her feet.

"We just came in for ice cream," Bella explained, noticing one of the bags had the logo of a maternity store. She recalled Blake mentioning that Jeanne was pregnant. "The stores here are out of my price range."

"Isn't my brother paying you enough?" Jeanne's question sounded like lighthearted teasing, but something beneath her tone raised Bella's defenses.

"He's paying me very well." She could see Jeanne's curiosity, but refused to explain further.

"Then you should be able to buy yourself a little something. I saw a darling dress at Martini's."

"I really can't."

"Well, if not an outfit for you—" Jeanne tugged Bella to her feet "—how about a toy for Drew?"

"He has more than he could ever play with," Bella protested, although she was less resistant to this suggestion.

"Have you been in the Pea Pod?" Jeanne gathered up her packages and sifted through the bags until she located the one she wanted. "I got this there." She showed off a colorful toy, rich with textures and interesting shapes. "You probably think it's crazy of me to buy toys when I've only just reached my second trimester, but shopping makes the time pass faster."

"Congratulations. Peter must be thrilled."

Jeanne made a face. "My husband is not like Blake. He's ambivalent at best about having a family. Not that he would ever say no to our having children," she hurried to explain. "It's just that he's not close with either of his brothers or his sister so he doesn't see how family benefits him."

Bella followed Jeanne across the street, pondering how important family was to Blake despite growing up with parents who hadn't been there for him and how she, who'd enjoyed a close relationship with her parents and siblings, had been determined never to have any children at all.

"That's the dress I was talking about," Jeanne said, pointing to a shop window. "I think it would be perfect on you."

Bella admired the party dress. It had a dark purple bodice with a gathered skirt that shaded to soft pink flowers at the hem.

"My sister would love it."

Bella smiled, imagining Jess's joy at receiving something so frivolously East Coast. Since Bella had moved to New York, her sister had become consumed with all things Manhattan. She'd watched every episode of *Sex and the City,* much to their mother's dismay, and imagined Bella living an exciting life of roaming around the city and hanging out with her fabulous friends in the gorgeous clothes that graced the glossy fashion magazines.

Of course, Jess knew that wasn't the reality, but she'd always been one to set her sights high. Her dream was to be a writer living in New York. She'd already had a couple stories published in small magazines. She planned to major in creative writing in college. Bella had little trouble imagining Jess succeeding in her goals.

"You should get it for her."

"She wouldn't have any place to wear it."

"She would if she came to visit you in New York."

"That won't happen until next summer. She's saving money for a plane ticket."

"Is it lonely being so far from home?"

"I miss my family, but I love living in New York."

"So you aren't going back to…where are you from?"

It was then that Bella realized Blake hadn't told his stepsister about his engagement. It might have upset her that he hadn't shared the news if she'd called Deidre or her family to tell them she was engaged. Normally she shared big news like hers right away. Instead, resistance rose inside her every time she went to dial home. It made her question if she was doing the right thing.

But how could marrying Blake be wrong? She loved him. She loved their son.

"I'm from Iowa. But I'm in New York to stay."

Bella continued down the street toward the store Jeanne had suggested they visit. The Pea Pod specialized in unique baby clothes as well as creative toys. She pushed the door open with her left hand and guided the stroller inside. As she held the door open for Blake's sister, she noticed Jeanne's attention snag on the four-carat diamond Blake had put on her finger yesterday.

"You're engaged?" Jeanne's tone held accusation as she glared at the ring. "To my brother?"

"Yes." At that second, Bella wished herself a hundred miles away. "He asked me yesterday."

Shock and disappointment reflected in Jeanne's expression. She was Victoria's best friend. Bella was certain Jeanne had been keen to have Victoria and Blake reconcile.

"Are you in love with him?"

"Of course." Bella couldn't believe the question. She yanked her hand free. "Why would you even ask that?"

"For someone like you, my brother must seem like a gold mine."

"I suppose that makes me a gold digger?" Shaking with suppressed fury, Bella still managed to keep her tone civil. "Do you think your brother is that gullible?"

Was this what Blake had been avoiding by not telling Jeanne about their engagement? No, Blake didn't dodge problems. He met them head-on. Bella was certain it was simply a timing issue between him and his stepsister.

"I think that because you were Drew's surrogate, Blake has a blind spot where you're concerned."

"Are you implying I would use Drew in some way to get to Blake?" Any joy she'd felt in the day was long gone. "That's not who I am."

Bella's throat closed over further words. She glanced around the store, reassured to see their discussion hadn't garnered any attention. Moving awkwardly in the tight space between displays, Bella navigated Drew's stroller until it was pointing toward the exit. Outside, Bella looked around, unsure where she'd left her car.

"I never said it was." Jeanne had followed her outside. "But aren't you moving too fast? You've only been back in Drew's life for a month."

"I love Drew."

"You abandoned him nine month ago."

Bella needed to get away from Blake's sister. She needed time to process what Jeanne was telling her. But as she headed back the way they'd come, Blake's stepsister was at her side. Feeling like a cornered animal, Bella rounded on her. "Victoria asked me to go. She said she and Blake needed time and space with Drew to become a family. So I left and I stayed away." At the end of the block she stopped to let several cars go before it was safe to cross.

"Does Blake know that?"

"I told him."

"No wonder he doesn't want to get back together with Victoria."

"There's more to their situation than that."

"Tell me."

Bella clamped her lips together and shook her head. "I've said enough. You need to get anything more from either Victoria or Blake."

"Then that's what I'll do." Jeanne stared at Bella a moment longer before turning on her heel and marching away.

Bella's gaze followed her. Was that what everyone in Blake's circle would assume? That she was marrying him for his money? The anonymity she'd enjoyed as a simple kindergarten teacher in New York City would be shattered as soon as news of their engagement reached the gossip columnists. It didn't take much imagination to picture the announcement on Page Six.

Wealthy CEO saves Iowa farm girl from a life of poverty by marrying her.

It would then be a short step to *Blake Ford weds son's surrogate*.

Hopefully by then they would become old news and the press wouldn't dig any deeper. Fertility clinics were supposed to be private, but there was no telling what an individual employee might be paid to reveal. Drew's true parentage might come to light.

Suddenly overwhelmed by the afternoon heat, Bella headed into the closest shop in search of some cooler air. Ironically, it was the boutique where Jeanne had seen the dress she thought would suit Bella.

The bell tinkled above the door, announcing Bella's entrance to the shop clerks. They gave her a once-over, but didn't approach. Her shorts and top weren't expensive enough to signal she was a serious shopper. Bella recognized the signs from when Deidre dragged her into the stores in Manhattan.

The air conditioning felt good against her overheated skin. She decided to take a closer look at the merchandise, specifically the dress displayed in the front window. Her target was on a rack near the front. Bella surreptitiously checked the price and sucked in a short, sharp breath. Four hundred dollars was a lot to spend. She stared at the garment and realized that soon she would be able to buy it without a second thought. Once she married Blake, there would no longer be a need to zealously guard every penny. The thought gave her pause.

The diamond on her finger felt heavier than ever. She glanced down at the sparkling token of Blake's promise and reminded herself she was marrying him in spite of his vast wealth. If it all vanished tomorrow she'd still want to be his wife. But that was unlikely to happen and questions crowded her. She didn't want to believe her motives were mercenary. She loved Blake. But money, or the lack of it, had been a burden for so long, she couldn't deny a small part of her wanted to buy things without checking a price tag or giving a single thought to where the money was going to come from.

In the end she left the store without making a purchase and returned to her car. Jeanne's words had bitten deeper than Bella had realized. She started the engine and headed back to the beach house.

Wasn't it enough for her to know she loved Blake and not his money? Did she really need the world to accept that as truth?

Blake was enjoying a vodka and tonic on the deck when he heard the front door close. He probably should have popped the cork on a bottle of champagne, such was the successful day he'd had, but that could wait until Drew was in bed. Then he and Bella could celebrate properly.

Listening to the brisk click of heels crossing the wood floor, he swung his feet off the lounge chair and stood. The woman passing through the living room was not the one he expected.

"Blake, where are you?"

He pushed open the sliding glass door and called to his stepsister. "Hello, Jeanne, what brings you here this afternoon?"

His stepsister whirled at the sound of his voice and

stormed toward him, outrage swirling around her like a cape. "You asked that girl to marry you?"

Her accusation made him realize he'd delayed too long informing her of his engagement. "If by *that girl* you mean Bella, then yes."

"You don't even know her." Instead of stopping when she reached where he stood, Jeanne began to pace along the windows.

"I've known her for almost two years. She is kind, nurturing and beautiful. Most importantly, she loves Drew."

"Don't you think you're moving way too fast?"

"When have you known me to do anything without thinking it through first?"

Jeanne's eyes flashed. "When you divorced Victoria."

"That decision was not made lightly." Blake kept his voice even as annoyance flared. "She gave me no choice."

"Why, because she didn't want to be a full-time mother?"

"There's more to it than that."

"What does that mean?"

Victoria might have felt okay about involving Jeanne in her campaign to reconcile and then pitting his sister against him when her plan failed, but Blake was not about to cause friction between the best friends by telling Jeanne all the reasons why their marriage had fallen apart.

"That means that Victoria hasn't told you the full story."

Uncertainty dampened Jeanne's irritation. "What is the full story?"

"She's your friend. Ask her."

"You're my brother. I'm asking you."

Blake crossed his arms and regarded his stepsister in determined silence until she growled his name. "I'm not going to involve you in a battle of he said, she said. Ask Victoria. If she chooses to tell you then you and I can discuss it further."

"And in the meantime you're planning on marrying Bella."

"I am." Blake led Jeanne to the couch and went to fetch a bottle of her favorite water. When he returned, she looked more troubled than angry. Handing her the bottle, he sat beside her on the sofa, his arm slung across the back, and waited for what was to come next.

Jeanne took a long sip of water and replaced the cap. "You don't think she's marrying you for your money?"

"Not in the least."

"But you paid her to be Drew's surrogate. You're paying her to be his nanny. Aren't you the least bit curious where all that money has gone?"

Blake's irritation faded to weariness. "This isn't any of your business, Jeanne."

"I'm your sister and I love you. Of course it's my business. What happened to all that money, Blake?"

"She sent it home," he told her, realizing Jeanne wasn't going to let up until she got answers. "To her parents, her brothers and sisters. Everything she can spare goes to help them out."

"So she says."

He shook his head. "It's the truth. I made my own inquiries."

"See," Jeanne exclaimed as if Blake had made her point for her. "You didn't trust her, either."

"Not after she refused to have any contact with Drew." Blake stared out the large windows at the far-off ocean. He liked the way the expansive view let his mind open to all sorts of possibilities. "But I've recently learned why that happened."

"She told me Victoria told her to stay away."

"Did she?" Blake shifted his attention back to Jeanne. "What else did she say?"

"That she loves you."

"Damn." He hadn't expected her to feel that way about

him. It was a precious burden he would carry the rest of his life.

"Do you love her?"

Bella froze at Jeanne's question. When she'd pulled into the driveway, she'd seen the familiar car parked by the front door and realized Jeanne must have raced over here as soon as she'd left Bella in town to tell Blake what a mistake he was making.

"What I feel doesn't matter," he said, his tone impatient.

Bella's heart constricted as it occurred to her that Blake had never spoken those three words. Deep down she'd feared being more emotionally invested in their relationship than Blake. It hurt to realize she'd been right.

"I loved Victoria," he continued, "and look how that turned out for Drew. She abandoned him to pursue her career. Much like my mother left me to return to Paris." A great deal of pain filled the silence that followed. No matter how perfect his life became, Blake would never fully get over his mother's abandonment. It afflicted every aspect of his personal life. "What is important is that Drew will have a mother who will care for him and love him completely."

Was that all Blake wanted from her? All the times they'd made love, the way he'd touched her with adoration as well as passion, was he only looking to cement her loyalty to him so she wouldn't ever leave?

"But why Bella? She's far from the most beautiful woman you've ever dated. Socially, she'll be utterly out of her element." Jeanne's comments echoed Bella's own worries. What would she talk to these people about? Her only contact with most of them was as a teacher. "There are a hundred women in Manhattan who would be a better choice for you and Drew."

"She's Drew's mother," Blake said firmly.

"Victoria is Drew's mother."

"She could have been, but she didn't want the role." And his tone said he didn't want to discuss the matter further. "And there's something else about the situation you don't understand."

Was Blake going to tell Jeanne about Victoria's infidelity? He sounded frustrated enough with his stepsister to set her straight on all counts.

"Like what?" Jeanne demanded.

"Bella is Drew's biological mother."

The shock of hearing this from Blake made Bella sway.

"That's impossible," Jeanne exclaimed. "She was just acting as Victoria's surrogate."

"It's true. I have billing statements from the fertility clinic as proof. Drew is not Victoria's biological son. He's Bella's."

Blake knew? How long? Why hadn't he said something to her about it?

Fearing she might drop Drew, she set him on the ground. He immediately began to crawl forward.

Blake spotted Drew about the same moment the little boy pulled himself to his feet with a happy cry and began toddling toward the kitchen. As if in slow motion, Bella watched his head swing from Drew toward her. She met his gaze, saw the determination in his eyes and for a second couldn't breathe.

Was that why he'd asked her to become his nanny? Why he'd sought her out? Why he'd asked her to marry him?

"Jeanne," he said, his voice low and even, his eyes never leaving Bella. "I think Bella and I need to talk in private."

"Sure." She sounded uncertain, as if the pressure in the room was set to explode at any moment. Moving with far less confident grace than usual, she left the sofa and circled around the room, giving Bella a wide berth.

The front door opened and closed.

Leaving Bella and Blake alone.

Twelve

"You knew?" Bella was shocked by how calm she sounded. "Why didn't you say something?" When Blake didn't answer her question immediately, she hit him with another. "Were you ever planning on telling me you knew? What would have happened when we had a second child and he looked exactly like Drew? Were you planning on ignoring that?"

"That's a question both of us should answer, don't you think?" Blake closed the distance until mere inches separated them. His voice lowered to a rumble. "Were you ever planning on telling me?"

Blood pounded in Bella's ears. Her earlier dizziness returned. What was she going to say to make this right?

"I don't know. Everything between us happened so fast. And then you proposed and..." Bella swayed forward and his arms came around her, a strong circle she never wanted to leave. "I was afraid I would lose you if I told you Drew was mine."

Heavy silence followed her declaration. As she waited for

Blake to decide whether to forgive her or send her packing, each second that ticked by was like another hole in the life raft that kept her from drowning.

"How long have you known?" she asked, muffling the question against his shoulder.

"A couple weeks."

Before he proposed to her.

Although it made her whole body ache to do so, Bella pushed out of Blake's arms. "That's why you want to marry me. Not because you love me. You told Jeanne you just wanted a mother for Drew. His real mother. Marrying someone you love wasn't in your plans."

"I'm sorry you overheard that."

But he wasn't sorry he felt that way.

"How long were you planning on keeping up the charade?" Bella demanded. "Did you think I wouldn't figure out eventually that ours wasn't a real marriage?"

"I care for you. I'm not pretending. You shouldn't be upset because I put Drew's needs above my own—when you left after he was born, you did the exact same thing. No matter how much it hurt to walk away."

"Does the thought of marrying me hurt?" Her voice sounded impossibly small, but it was hard speaking past the tightness in her throat and chest.

"Don't be ridiculous. I'm thrilled that we're going to be a family."

"But you don't love me."

"Stop harping on that."

"But it's important to me. The reason I resisted having children for so long is that I was afraid to be trapped in a situation like my mother was. There were so many of us to take care of. There was never enough money. She seemed exhausted and worried all the time. I didn't want that for myself. I refused ever to settle for less than what made me happy."

"What are you saying?"

"That I now find myself trapped in an untenable situation. I can't marry you knowing that you don't love me, but I want more than anything to be Drew's mother."

"But you could marry me knowing that I will be forever faithful as well as grateful for the gift of Drew and any other children we might have."

Grateful?

Bella crossed her arms to ward off a sudden chill. Could she be happy with half a marriage? It was unrealistic to believe that anyone enjoyed a life of complete bliss, but for two short days she'd thought Blake loved her and she'd never been happier. Sure, she'd had a few concerns, but not when Blake held her in his arms. Not when she snuggled Drew.

"I need some time to think."

She eased sideways in the direction of the stairs, tugging off the expensive ring as she went. As it came free of her finger, a burden seemed to lift off her shoulders. Marrying Blake had been a pipe dream. She'd been a fool to think he could love her. Now she'd never have to struggle to make herself acceptable to his friends or worry that they would believe she'd married him for his money.

Blake caught her wrist before she could set the ring down on a nearby table. His grip was firm, but not painful. "Keep the ring. It's a symbol of how much I want us to be a family."

"If you're worried that I'm going to abandon Drew," she said, "don't be. I don't need a ring or a marriage proposal to keep me around. I love Drew. He's the most important person in my life. I'd never turn my back on him."

"What about me? Do you think I proposed marriage on a whim? I want you in my life, as well. This last month I realized just how important you are to me."

With a strong tug, Bella freed her wrist and pressed the ring into Blake's palm, closing his fingers around it. "I couldn't be happy knowing I was standing in the way of you finding someone you love and making a life with her.'

Then, with her sight blurred by tears, Bella raced upstairs, leaving behind the two men she loved most in the world.

Blake stared after Bella until a crash sounded behind him. Drew's wail erupted a second later. He'd jostled an end table and caused a picture frame to fall. Blake scooped him off the floor and saw that he wasn't hurt, just startled.

With his son riding his shoulders, Blake strode upstairs. His conversation with Bella had been a disaster, but Blake wasn't ready to just let all his plans fall apart. Her bedroom door was closed, signaling she wasn't in the mood to talk. He considered knocking for a brief moment before Drew began to yawn. His son needed a diaper change and a nap. There would be time to approach Bella after Drew was asleep.

But by the time Drew was settled, Bella was in the midst of packing.

"Where do you think you're going?" Blake demanded, unsettled by this new development.

"I need some time to think. So I thought I'd go home for a few days."

"I'll make arrangements for you to fly back to New York. Will four days be enough time? We're supposed to attend the Weavers' anniversary party."

"I'm not going to New York. I'm heading back to Iowa."

She'd told him she was returning home after Drew's birth and then she ended up staying in New York. This time he believed she was going to Iowa. He was less confident she would be coming back.

"What's a few days?"

"Five. Maybe a week."

Was he on the brink of losing her all over again? "Drew will miss you if you're gone too long."

"I know. But he has you. And Jeanne and Mrs. Farnes."

"That's not the same as having his mother."

"I'm not leaving forever, Blake. It's just a week."

"Why don't you stay here and think. If it's space you need, I can return to New York. I'll take Drew with me if you'd like."

She shook her head. "I can't let you leave your home. Don't worry about me. I'll be fine."

He'd met this same wall of stubborn determination after Drew was born, when she'd refused contact with him. The familiarity of the situation put him on edge.

"You'll call me?"

"Of course." She zipped up her suitcase and slipped her purse over her shoulder. "Now I really need to get going. There's a bus heading back to New York in an hour."

"I'll drive you into town."

"No need. I've ordered a taxi."

Suddenly Blake couldn't bear to let her go. "Stay."

"I can't. Not right now."

He stepped into her path and cupped her face in his hands, holding her steady while his lips dipped to hers. He kissed her as if she was the only woman for him and she responded in kind, but in the end, she was still holding on to the handle of her suitcase, and the way she averted her gaze said she was still determined to make her bus.

"Come back to us," Blake told her.

"I will." But her expression was sad rather than reassuring. "Goodbye, Blake. Give Drew a kiss for me. Tell him…" A gentle smile flitted across her lips. "Elephant shoes."

A heartbeat later she was gone.

And Blake was left feeling that this time it was no one's fault but his that the most important woman in his life was walking away.

When Bella entered the apartment she shared with Deidre, her roommate was waiting. Bella had called from the bus, saying she was coming home, but didn't get into detail about what happened.

"Are you okay?" Deidre opened her arms and swallowed Bella in a tight embrace.

It was hard to maintain an unflappable demeanor with so much sympathy and understanding pouring down on her. The emotional outburst she'd kept locked inside the entire afternoon burst free. Sobs wrenched at her. All the disappointment and hurt at finding out that Blake didn't love her tore her apart until Bella was certain she'd never feel whole again.

When at last she'd gotten past the worst of it, Deidre spoke.

"What happened?"

"Blake knew I was Drew's biological mom."

"Was he angry?"

"No." She'd been so convinced that if he found out about how she and Victoria had deceived him he would never want to speak to her again. "I think he's known for a while."

"Did Victoria tell him?"

Bella shook her head. "He said something about having a medical bill from the fertility clinic?"

"Why is this a big deal?" Deidre knew only that Bella and Blake had been intimate. Now her friend needed to hear the rest of the story.

"He asked me to marry him." She rubbed her bare ring finger. "We were engaged for two whole days."

"What?" Deidre erupted in shocked tones. "And you didn't immediately call and tell me?"

"I didn't tell anyone."

"Not even your family?"

Bella rubbed a new batch of tears from her cheeks. "No. And I can't explain why. I think maybe I was afraid something like this would happen."

"Who broke off the engagement?"

"I did."

"Why?"

"Because he's only marrying me because I'm Drew's mother. He doesn't love me."

"Did he tell you that before or after you agreed to marry him?"

Bella hit her roommate with a hard expression. "I found out today. And as soon as I did, I broke off the engagement. How am I supposed to marry him knowing he only wanted me around for my maternal instincts?"

"Oh, I can see where being married to a handsome, charming billionaire would be one of the worst things that could happen to a girl," Deidre taunted. "But do you really expect me to believe that a man who could have any woman in Manhattan would settle for a loveless marriage for the sake of his son?" She shook her head. "I don't see it."

"But that's exactly what he wanted."

"You said you two were sensational together in bed. It can't be that great without some emotional connection."

Deidre's arguments weren't helping Bella's peace of mind.

"Well, sure, we like each other."

"You were marrying a man you only liked?"

Bella's breath gusted out. "Okay, I'm in love with him."

"Madly? Passionately?"

"Deeply. Irrevocably."

"So, the man you adore—the father of the baby you've been missing like crazy for almost a year—likes you and wants to marry you." Deidre paused and waited for Bella's reluctant nod. "And you turned him down because it's not enough?"

"Put that way, I sound like a complete idiot."

"Not an idiot. But you do sound afraid. Haven't you spent your whole life running from anything that you didn't think was perfect? Your mother's choices are not ones you would have made, but from what you've told me, she's completely happy with her life."

"I've been thinking a lot about that. I think I've been so determined not to have children because I'm just like her and I know once I got started, I'd want to keep going until eventually I'd be financially strapped and tied down with no hope of getting free."

"That doesn't have to be what happens to you. Marry Blake and you'll have more money than you can spend and an army of nannies to take care of your brood."

Deidre's pragmatism echoed what Jeanne had said. She glared at her friend. "And have everyone assume I'm only marrying him for his money?"

"Why do you care what anyone thinks? As long as your motives are pure, they can all go jump off a bridge." Deidre went to the kitchen and came back with two glasses filled with red wine. "We are going to drink this wonderful Cab I got from my friend Tony and then you are going to tell me what club you'd like to hit tonight. Before you decide Blake isn't the one for you, I suggest you remember what life is like as a single girl. Then you can tell me if that's really what you want."

"What if it is?"

"Then I'll support you one hundred percent. But if it's not, I expect you to call Blake and tell him you want a long engagement followed by a sensational New York City wedding with all the trimmings." Deidre held out her hand. "Deal?"

Wondering what sort of trimmings Deidre was talking about, Bella shook her roommate's hand. "Deal."

The beach house echoed with loneliness. Blake sat in the darkness, an untouched tumbler of scotch at his elbow, and stared out into the night. Bella had been gone for three days.

Blake woke every morning to an empty bed and a sick feeling in his gut. Nor was he the only one to feel the impact of Bella's absence. Drew was fussier than ever. Exhausting himself by crying for hours at night and then refusing to settle down for naptime. If Blake thought his son was too young to notice that Bella wasn't around, he'd misjudged the bond that had formed between mother and son.

She hadn't answered any of his numerous phone calls, but had texted him that she was fine and simply needed some time and space to think. He was beginning to worry she wouldn't come back to them. No, he amended. She would return and take up her role as Drew's mother. She loved her son and would fight to stay in his life.

Even if that meant suffering a relationship with Blake to do it.

His cell rang. Heart leaping in joy, he checked the display, but it was only Jeanne.

"We are having a few people over for dinner, tonight," she told him, her tone authoritative. "You should join us."

"I'm not sure that's a good idea."

"Bring Bella. I'm sure Mrs. Farnes wouldn't mind watching Drew tonight."

"Bella's not here." He wanted to blame Jeanne for his predicament, but in all fairness, couldn't pass on the blame for Bella's leaving. "She went home to Iowa for a week or so."

"Is everything all right?" Jeanne's concern came through the phone.

"I don't know. She won't answer my calls."

"Is this because she overheard our conversation?"

"What do you think?"

"I think you're annoyed with me," Jeanne retorted. "It's not my fault that Bella left. You are the one who proposed to her under false pretenses."

"They weren't false. I intended for us to be a family. I wouldn't ever do anything to hurt her or make her regret marrying me."

"And there's nothing you can do about that tonight. Come have dinner with us."

"Another night."

Blake hung up on his stepsister. He was unfit company for anyone.

Less than ten minutes later, his doorbell rang. Cursing, he went to answer, expecting Jeanne, but it was Victoria who stood on his doorstep.

"If you've come to persuade me to have dinner at Jeanne's, you are wasting your breath."

"That's not why I'm here." Victoria strode past him into the home they'd shared for five years. "Jeanne said you hadn't taken down any of the pictures of me until the beginning of summer."

"Don't read anything into it."

"Have you asked yourself why?"

"Because I hadn't gotten around to it."

"I think there's a lot more to it than that." Vicky gave him a crafty smile as she took the glass he offered. "Jeanne said you and Bella are getting married."

"Did she also tell you that she and I are having problems?"

"She said you don't love her."

"I loved you and look how our marriage turned out."

"Do you think a marriage without love will have better luck?" Victoria quizzed. "Or are you afraid to fail at love a second time?"

Her question cut him. "I'm putting Drew's needs before my own."

"That's not going to work for you."

For the better part of the past five days, he'd pondered his marriage to Vicky and the way things had gone downhill toward the end. He could blame her for choosing her career over Drew, and her disinterest in being a mother had definitely led to trouble between them, but he'd married her knowing how much she identified with being a model.

He'd been proud of her ambition. Enjoyed how she'd looked on his arm. Disregarded her insecurity as the modeling jobs dried up. She was beautiful and self-centered, exciting and infuriating. Demanding his complete attention and sulking when she didn't receive it. Keeping her happy had required a great deal of his energy and there were days when he didn't even try. They hadn't had a partnership. They'd had a nonstop power struggle.

Being with Vicky had been exciting, but many days had felt joyless. There had been weeks when being married reminded him of the loneliness he'd felt as a child when his mother stayed in Paris for long periods of time.

"Did you know I told Bella never to contact us after Drew was born?"

"She told me." He wondered where his ex-wife was going with her confession. "She said it was because having her around would create confusion and complications for Drew."

"Partly. Mostly I hated the way you two got along. She was happy to listen to you talk about your business. The same things that bored me to death fascinated her. She made you laugh. You ate up the stories of her family. When you two were together, I felt like an outsider."

"We were friends," Blake protested. "Nothing more."

"It was a lot. You two connected in a way that we never did. I didn't like it."

"I wasn't interested in her beyond simple friendship."

"Because you and I were married and you are an honorable man. But she was in love with you. It was obvious to me. So I asked her to leave us in peace."

Blake couldn't believe what he was hearing. "She was not in love with me."

"From the start, I think. And who could blame her? I fell for you the first night we went out."

"Why are you telling me this?"

"Because you're not in love with her and that's going to break her heart one day. Do you really want to do that to her?"

The news that Bella had once been in love with him dominated his attention. Blake heard Vicky continuing the conversation, but her words were indistinct. Was that the way Bella still felt? And he'd just let her go? Would she ever forgive him?

"Even though you and I want different things, when my play failed, all I wanted to do was run back and have you take care of me the way you used to."

But he didn't want to take care of Vicky any longer. She'd chosen her career over being a family with him. Her lies and infidelity might have put an end to their marriage, but it had been in trouble for a long time before that.

"You and I are done," he told her, getting to his feet.

Not once in the month that he'd been with Bella had he longed for something different or better. Her even temper, quick mind and dry sense of humor made her wonderful company. She took care of everyone around her and didn't expect anything in return. He'd been a skeptical fool to think she'd refuse contact with Drew because she didn't care about him. In truth, she'd cared too much.

Loving her was easy. Comfortable. Being with her brought him utter contentment. He hadn't recognized the sensation as love because that wasn't how love had been for him growing up. The love he'd known made him feel empty. Alone. He'd never known completeness.

He'd never known real love.

Blake plucked the glass from Vicky's hand and tugged her to her feet. He loved Bella. Her sweetness. Her passion. Her sunny disposition and her stubbornness. She might be afraid to acknowledge it, but she wanted what he did: a family. Someone to love and sacrifice for. Someone who would be there when you needed them.

Ignoring his ex-wife's sputtering protests, he guided her firmly toward the front door. "Vicky, you are not the woman I want to be with anymore."

Her eyes narrowed in icy calculation. "You're serious about marrying that farm girl? Think about your friends. They'll never accept her. Your lifestyle in New York City. She'll do nothing but make a fool of herself at the events you attend."

"Bella is everything I could want in a woman. If my friends don't like her, I need new friends. And I only went to the parties because you insisted we had to be seen. I intend to be there for my son in a way my father wasn't." To ensure that Vicky understood this wasn't a game and that he actually wanted her gone, Blake walked her out to her car. "I wish you all the best."

But his ex-wife wasn't done. "You're making a huge mistake."

"The only mistake I've made is not realizing sooner that I'm in love with Bella." He opened Vicky's car door and gestured her in. "But I've finally come to my senses and I have you to thank."

He didn't linger to watch his ex-wife drive off. He had plans to make. Disturbed that he'd let Bella leave thinking he didn't love her, Blake knew he had to do something to win her back. But what? Impressing her with a grand financial gesture would not be the best way to apologize. Anything he did would have to come from the heart. For a man who was able to buy everything he needed, this was a daunting realization.

The first thing he needed to do was head to Iowa and meet her family. He never should have proposed to her without seeing where she was from and getting acquainted with the people who knew her best.

Despite the late hour, Blake contacted his personal assistant and got her started making arrangements. Then he headed upstairs to pack and figure out what he could do for the woman who never seemed to want anything for herself.

* * *

The next morning Blake and Drew headed for Iowa. He would do whatever it took to win Bella back. He loved her. Could he convince her that he'd been a fool or would she simply believe that he was saying what she wanted to hear?

In Dubuque, he rented a car and drove the hour and a half to the town where Bella had been born. With each mile that passed, the declarations he went over in his head grew less eloquent. By the time he turned onto the long driveway that would take him to the house, Blake had only pleading left in his arsenal.

With a family as large as Bella's, a strange car approaching the house was cause for curiosity. As the vehicle rolled to a stop, he was surrounded by two dogs, a goat and four children ranging in age from about five to the midteens.

Blake exited the car, stretching as his feet hit the gravel driveway, and smiled in as friendly a manner as possible. "Hello," he said. "I'm Blake Ford. I'm here to see Bella."

"She's in New York," one of the boys said.

"Why do you want to see Bella?"

A dog drew close and growled.

"She told me she was coming home for a visit."

"We haven't seen her since Christmas," the oldest girl said. "Is that your baby?"

"Yes." Before Blake could stop her, she'd opened the car door and unfastened him from the seat. "His name is Drew."

"He looks exactly like Ben when he was a baby."

"I'm sure all babies look alike."

"Maybe." The girl carried Drew toward the house. "Come inside and I'll show you Ben's baby pictures. You'll see for yourself."

Blake trailed after the girl. As they neared the farmhouse, a woman stepped through the screen door. She dried her hands on a dishcloth and looked from Blake to Drew.

"Hello," he said, coming forward to offer her his hand. "I'm Blake Ford. We spoke on the phone a month ago."

"I remember," the woman said, taking Drew from her daughter. "You said Bella took care of your son. Is this him?"

"Yes."

"Mama, don't you think he looks like Ben when he was a baby?"

"He does." Bella's mother fastened a hard look on Blake. "Why is that, Mr. Ford?"

"I think that's something we should go inside and discuss."

Thirteen

It only took one night of clubbing with Deidre for Bella to realize this wasn't what she should be doing. They were out until dawn, going from club to party to breakfast with some of Deidre's friends. By the time Bella fell into bed at five in the morning, she'd wished a hundred times that she'd spent the evening with Blake and Drew.

During the trip back to the city, she'd decided against going to Iowa. Her family's farm wasn't where she belonged anymore. Home was wherever Drew lived.

While she struggled against what her heart told her to do, Bella moped around her apartment. Restless, edgy, eating little, sleeping badly, by the fifth night, Bella's nerves were stretched thin.

She lay awake, staring at her ceiling, watching the day brighten and feeling as if she'd made nothing but a series of bad decisions. Yesterday, Deidre had sat her down for a reality check. Her roommate made a great deal of sense. There was no perfect relationship. If she spent her life chasing after one, she'd probably end up miserable and alone.

But could she marry Blake and be a family with him and Drew knowing that he didn't love her?

Yes.

Being with him and Drew had made her happy this summer. Deep down she'd known he didn't love her, but she'd been more content than ever before. She belonged with Drew. And with Blake.

The bus trip back to the Hamptons seemed endless, offering her way too much time to rehearse what she was going to say to Blake. She imagined a dozen scenarios. Each one ended with Blake throwing her out of the house and telling her never to return.

Telling the taxi driver to wait, Bella headed up the front walk to the beach house. She rang the bell rather than use her key. Blake might be more receptive to her return if she didn't barge in with a presumptuous air.

Mrs. Farnes answered the door and looked surprised to see Bella. "You're here?"

Bella's heart sank. "I came to see Blake."

"He's not here."

"Did he return to New York?" She should have called before making the trip, but what she had to say needed to be said in person. She couldn't risk Blake hanging up on her before she'd spoken her heart.

Mrs. Farnes stepped back and gestured Bella inside. "He's in Iowa." The housekeeper looked amused. "Visiting you."

"But I didn't go to Iowa." She thought of all those phone calls from Blake that she'd not answered and her spirits rose. "How long has he been gone?"

"He left yesterday morning."

That meant he'd been with her family for almost twenty-four hours. "I'd better call him."

Bella returned to the taxi and paid the driver. For the moment she wasn't going anywhere. On her way back inside the beach house, she dialed Blake. He answered on the third ring.

"Where are you?" he demanded.

His concerned tone set her heart to pounding madly. "I'm at the beach house. Where are you?"

"At your family's farm. I'm helping your father repair the tractor. Apparently the starter has been giving him trouble."

"Why are you there?"

"Because this is where you said you were coming." Blake spoke to someone in the background before returning to their conversation. "What are you doing at the beach house?"

"I thought you'd be here and I came back to tell you that I'm sorry I left the way I did. I want you, Drew and me to be a family if you still want me."

"I chased after you all the way to Iowa." Blake's deep voice took on a somber note. "Of course I want you. If we were in the same state, I'd show you just how much."

Helpless laughter seized Bella. "We have terrible timing, don't we?"

"I think both of us have been afraid to acknowledge what we really want for fear of being hurt."

Bella was impressed by his insight. "I'm not afraid anymore. That's what I came here to tell you. For so long I've been running from what I wanted most—a family. I thought it would be a burden, not a joy."

"The way I proposed to you was so wrong. I should never have let you believe I was only thinking of Drew. The truth is I could have found any number of women who would have made Drew a good mother. Not one of them would have been the wife for me. Only you. It was awfully convenient that you were Drew's biological mom because it gave me a way to make us a family without having to admit that I was the one who couldn't live without you."

Tears wound their way down Bella's cheeks. "Damn you, Blake. Why do you have to be so far away?"

"Whatever impulse you're feeling, hang on to it. I'll be there in six hours to pick you up and bring you back."

"You don't need to do that. I can fly commercial."

"Don't be ridiculous. I'll call you en route to tell you what time we're going to land."

"Please hurry," Bella murmured, too overcome by emotion to be able to speak louder than a whisper. "I've really missed you."

"Elephant shoes," Blake said in return. "See you in a few hours."

Bella stared at the now silent phone. "He loves me." She looked up and realized Mrs. Farnes was returning from the kitchen, a cup of hot tea in her hand. "He loves me," she repeated, still stunned by the realization.

"Of course he does," said the housekeeper with a broad smile. "That's been obvious for a long time."

As soon as the Gulfstream touched down and rolled to a halt at East Hampton Airport, Blake was on his feet and waiting at the door for his crew to lower the stairs. With the way cleared, he rushed down, eyes scanning the hangar for Bella. She stood off to one side, her suitcase at her feet, blue eyes seeming larger than ever in her pale face.

Her uncertainty touched him. She wanted so badly to make others happy that most times she forgot about her own needs. He would spend the rest of his life making sure she lacked for nothing.

Half a dozen long strides brought him within reach. He snatched her off her feet and swung her in a wide circle. Her laugh bounced off the walls of the hangar as she clutched at his shoulders. As soon as he set her down, his mouth captured hers in a long, hungry kiss that disclosed his feelings for her.

"I missed you," he said at long last, framing her face with his hands while he refreshed his memories of her features.

"I missed you, too." She gave him a shy smile. "And I can't wait to see Drew."

"It's going to be a couple hours until that happens. I left him with your family."

"You left him?" She looked horrified. "Do you realize my dad will probably take him for a ride on the tractor? Or one of my brothers might think it's a great idea to introduce him to the calves. Or the girls will make him play tea party. There's no telling what could happen."

Blake gave her an odd look. "I'm sure he'll be fine. I thought you and I could use a few hours to ourselves." He picked up her suitcase and wrapped his arm around her waist. "By the way, your mother figured out Drew is your son."

Bella stumbled, but Blake's arm kept her stable and she quickly recovered. "How?"

"Apparently he looks just like Ben did when he was a baby."

"That's impossible. Drew takes after you."

"Not according to your family. And I've seen the pictures. They're right. He has the McAndrews chin and nose."

"Did you explain to your mother what happened?"

"Since I'm unsure on all the details, I thought it would be better if you told her." It was a gentle nudge to share the story with him.

As soon as they sat down on the plane, Bella snuggled beside Blake in one of the comfortable leather chairs, her head on his shoulder.

"How did you find out that Victoria isn't Drew's mother?"

"I came across some of the paperwork from the clinic. The treatment was a lot less expensive than it should have been. When I looked at the itemized statement, I noticed that the charges weren't for in vitro, but for artificial insemination."

"Victoria told me her eggs weren't viable," Bella explained, remembering her shock when the former model had asked to use Bella's eggs as well as have her carry the baby.

"As far as I know that's not true," Blake said.

"I guess I'm just a gullible farm girl from Iowa." Bella burned with humiliation at being so easily duped. "I believed her."

"My ex-wife excelled at telling a person what they wanted to hear." There was a hint of frustration beneath Blake's even tone. "For years she let me believe she wanted to have a family."

"Maybe she didn't know what she wanted until it was too late," she suggested. "I know that she was determined to hold on to you."

"Is that how she talked you into letting us use one of your eggs?"

"She was frantic, telling me that your marriage would be over because she couldn't give you a baby. It was entirely plausible. Infertility can tear apart a marriage."

"But how did she think she could get away with lying to me about our son's parentage?"

"Desperate people do foolish things sometimes." Bella stared up at his strong profile, saw the muscle move in his cheek. "I should know. I gave away my son in exchange for the money to help my parents keep their farm."

Blake cupped her cheek in his hand and kissed her with slow, thorough adoration. "And every day that goes by I thank heavens your parents had financial difficulties, because otherwise we never would have met and I wouldn't have my son."

"I'm not sure they'd appreciate hearing you say that," Bella teased, sliding her hand along his muscular arm, enjoying the strength of him beneath her fingertips.

"They're going to be my family now. I hope you realize I'm going to take good care of all your siblings."

Bella groaned. "Please don't tell them that. They already see me as the cash cow. If they have any idea how generous you are, they'll never leave you alone."

"Don't worry. I can handle them." His lips covered hers, silencing any further protest she might make.

Relaxing into the familiar press and retreat of his kiss, Bella hummed in appreciation of the masterful way he could make her forget everything but what was happening at that moment. For too long she'd worried about the future. Blake kept her completely grounded in the present.

"I love the sounds you make," he murmured, gliding his lips along her neck.

She shivered in delight as he lightly sucked on her sensitive skin. "What sounds?"

"Your moans have terrific range. They tell me how much you like something. And then there's the way you purr. I know you're really happy when that happens."

"I do all that?" Despite the level of physical intimacy she'd experienced with him, hearing his praise sent heat spiraling into her cheeks.

"All that and more." He kissed her forehead. "You make me happier than I've ever been."

Was that possible? His marriage to Victoria had seemed perfect. They'd been an it couple. Attractive, talented, wealthy. Bella couldn't remember a time when they were in the same room and didn't touch in some way. She'd envied their obvious passion for each other.

"I'm glad."

Blake's intent blue eyes grew sharp. "You don't sound convinced."

"You forget, I saw you with Victoria."

"She didn't make me feel like you do. Living with her was often exhausting. She loved drama. When it didn't present itself organically, she created it."

"But you seemed so happy."

"Our marriage worked as long as Victoria got what she wanted. And I was happy to give her whatever. All I wanted was for us to be parents. Things began to change as soon as she agreed to try for a baby."

Bella kept silent. The best thing she could do was trust that Blake knew what he was getting into by marrying her. He was telling her that he was tired of beautiful and exciting. He wanted…what? Plain and dull? She sighed.

"With you, I feel as if we're a partnership," he continued. "So you can stop sighing. It's great with you. I know we're on the same page."

"Are you sure you're not going to be…"

"Bored?"

His knack for reading her mind never ceased to surprise her. "You might miss all the drama."

A slow smile spread across his lips. "I'll take your brand of passion over Vicky's love of chaos any day."

And the hot, sexy kiss he planted on her demonstrated just how true that was.

Bella expected a mob scene when she arrived at her parents' farm and her family didn't disappoint her. The last time she'd been home was for a week at Christmas. The crowded, noisy farmhouse had seemed claustrophobic after her quiet apartment in New York. Plus, she'd been unable to answer their questions about what she'd been doing during the year since she'd last visited.

More than anything she'd wanted to be able to share the truth with her mother. Giving up Drew had been an open wound and she longed for nothing more than to sob out her pain in her mother's arms. But taking comfort was something she'd never learned how to do. It was always her supporting others. So she'd put on a brave face and bottled up her sadness.

"You're home." Jess was the first to reach her. As soon as Blake stopped the car, Bella's sister yanked open the door and wrapped her arms around Bella, practically falling into her lap as she did so. "I missed you," she said softly.

"Me, too," Bella whispered back.

Blake stuck close to her side as they entered the house, his fingers entwined with hers. He was a solid buffer against her boisterous family as they pummeled her with dozens of questions she didn't know how to answer.

"I'd like to see Drew," she told him, angling toward the stairs.

"Your mother put him in your old room. When Drew and I arrived, she insisted we spend the night here rather than in town."

Bella nodded. "There's only two motels and neither one is up to your standards." She entered her old room and saw immediately that Jess had taken over the space. As the oldest girl still living at home, it made sense that she would get it. "Oh, look. He's awake."

Drew was standing in the crib, his chubby fists gripping the railing. He bounced excitedly when he spotted her.

"He looks none the worse for wear," Blake said. "Your family didn't play too rough."

It wasn't until Bella had him in her arms that the tension of the past week melted away. How had she been stupid enough to walk away from Drew twice? "I'll never leave you again," she murmured into the baby's soft neck.

"Blake, would it be all right if I had a moment alone with my daughter?"

"Certainly."

Turning around, Bella saw her mother in the doorway. Remembering what Blake had told her as they boarded the plane, her stomach twisted into knots of dread. As soon as they were alone, Bella sat down on the bed, Drew cradled against her chest like a shield.

"I know what you're going to say," she began.

"Do you?" Her mother sat down on the bed beside her. "What exactly am I going to say?"

"You are going to tell me what I did was thoughtless and wrong."

"Since I'm not exactly sure what you did, that's not what I was going to say at all." Her mother cupped Drew's head with gentle fingers. "How did all this come to be?"

"When I went to New York, I went there to answer an ad placed by a firm that matched infertile couples with surrogates." When her mother didn't react, Bella continued. "That's where I met Blake. He and his wife were having trouble conceiving and so they decided to use a surrogate."

"But usually a surrogate doesn't supply the egg, correct?"

"Victoria told me her eggs were no good."

"She told you?" Bella's mother echoed. "Was that the case?"

Bella shook her head. "At the time all I knew was that she was desperate to save her marriage by having a baby. I felt sorry for her so I...helped."

"Bella." Her mother sounded aghast. "That was your child you were giving up."

"You didn't see the expression on Blake's face the day he took me for the ultrasound. He was thrilled I was carrying his son. I knew at that moment that I would do anything to make him happy, even sacrifice my own happiness by never seeing Drew ever again so that Blake and Victoria could be the happy family he wanted." Bella kissed Drew's head. "Besides, I'd never planned on having any children. It never occurred to me I would get so attached."

"When did you realize something changed?"

"The first time I felt him kick. By then it was too late. And Blake was so excited about becoming a father."

"Are you in love with him?"

"More than anything."

"He asked your father permission to marry you."

"Really?" Bella was utterly charmed that Blake would do something so old-fashioned. It wasn't what she would have expected.

"Are you going to marry him?"

"I don't know." She grinned at her mother. "Did Dad say yes or no?"

"That's between them." Her mother was silent for a long time. "You probably don't think I've realized just how much you've done for this family."

Bella scrunched up her face. "I would do whatever I could to help you."

"You've given more than your fair share of time and money to help us out. That stops now. Living in New York City isn't the dream I had for you, but I can see Blake and Drew make you happy. I'm glad you found a man who loves you the way your father loves me."

And love was what made her mother's burden lighter, Bella realized. Love for her husband. His for her. The love she had for the farm and her children. The financial struggles, the vast amount of work that needed to be done on a daily basis, the petty spats between her kids, all of that rolled off Stella's back because she was happy with the life she'd chosen.

What a blessing that was.

"It's time for you to get a little selfish," her mother continued. "Promise me you'll put yourself first at least once a week."

Blake appeared in the doorway and grinned at both women. "I intend to take excellent care of her."

Bella's mother smiled. "It's nice to see someone worrying about you for a change." She stood and plucked Drew from his mother's arms. "I'm going to take Drew downstairs and find him a snack."

Once they were alone, Blake came to kneel beside Bella. He pulled out the diamond ring she'd returned to him earlier that week. "The last time I did this all wrong. I'd like to try again."

Nodding, unable to speak past the lump in her throat, Bella stared at the ring Blake slipped on her finger.

"Bella McAndrews, I love you with all my heart. Will you do me the honor of becoming my wife?"

She slid her hands around his neck and leaned forward until their lips were inches apart. "Blake Ford, you are my heart and my life. I will marry you and spend the rest of my days making you happy."

A reverent kiss sealed their commitment to each other. When Blake released her, Bella's whole body was tingling with passion and joy.

"Shall we go tell your family the news?"

"I'm sure three of them are outside the door listening to us," she retorted, kissing him hard and fast. "In this house there is no privacy."

Blake stood. "Then perhaps we should go downstairs and accept their congratulations."

"We should." She let him pull her to her feet.

As they left her childhood bedroom, Bella thought back over all the nights she'd lain here and plotted how her life would go. Not once had she contemplated living in New York City, being married to a billionaire and raising a family.

With her fingers laced with Blake's, she marveled at how despite her best efforts to avoid it, she'd gotten what her heart truly wanted all along.

* * * * *

And if you liked this BILLIONAIRES & BABIES *novel, watch for the next book in this #1 bestselling series, coming next month: YULETIDE BABY SURPRISE by USA TODAY bestselling author Catherine Mann*

REQUEST YOUR FREE BOOKS!
2 FREE NOVELS PLUS 2 FREE GIFTS!

HARLEQUIN®

Desire

ALWAYS POWERFUL, PASSIONATE AND PROVOCATIVE

YES! Please send me 2 FREE Harlequin Desire® novels and my 2 FREE gifts (gifts are worth about $10). After receiving them, if I don't wish to receive any more books, I can return the shipping statement marked "cancel." If I don't cancel, I will receive 6 brand-new novels every month and be billed just $4.55 per book in the U.S. or $4.99 per book in Canada. That's a savings of at least 13% off the cover price! It's quite a bargain! Shipping and handling is just 50¢ per book in the U.S. and 75¢ per book in Canada.* I understand that accepting the 2 free books and gifts places me under no obligation to buy anything. I can always return a shipment and cancel at any time. Even if I never buy another book, the two free books and gifts are mine to keep forever.

225/326 HDN F4ZC

Name _____ (PLEASE PRINT) _____

Address _____ Apt. # _____

City _____ State/Prov. _____ Zip/Postal Code _____

Signature (if under 18, a parent or guardian must sign)

Mail to the **Harlequin® Reader Service:**
IN U.S.A.: P.O. Box 1867, Buffalo, NY 14240-1867
IN CANADA: P.O. Box 609, Fort Erie, Ontario L2A 5X3

Want to try two free books from another line?
Call 1-800-873-8635 or visit www.ReaderService.com.

* Terms and prices subject to change without notice. Prices do not include applicable taxes. Sales tax applicable in N.Y. Canadian residents will be charged applicable taxes. Offer not valid in Quebec. This offer is limited to one order per household. Not valid for current subscribers to Harlequin Desire books. All orders subject to credit approval. Credit or debit balances in a customer's account(s) may be offset by any other outstanding balance owed by or to the customer. Please allow 4 to 6 weeks for delivery. Offer available while quantities last.

Your Privacy—The Harlequin® Reader Service is committed to protecting your privacy. Our Privacy Policy is available online at www.ReaderService.com or upon request from the Harlequin Reader Service.

We make a portion of our mailing list available to reputable third parties that offer products we believe may interest you. If you prefer that we not exchange your name with third parties, or if you wish to clarify or modify your communication preferences, please visit us at www.ReaderService.com/consumerschoice or write to us at Harlequin Reader Service Preference Service, P.O. Box 9062, Buffalo, NY 14269. Include your complete name and address.

HD13R

SPECIAL EXCERPT FROM

What will happen when this beauty tries to tame the beast?

*Here's a sneak peek at the next book in
Andrea Laurence's SECRETS OF EDEN miniseries,
A BEAUTY UNCOVERED, coming
October 2013 from Harlequin® Desire.*

Brody turned on his heel, ready to return to his office and lick his wounds, when she called out to him again.

"Mr. Eden?"

"Yes?" He stopped and faced her.

Sam rounded her desk and approached him. His body tensed involuntarily as she came closer. She reached up to the scarred side of his face, causing his lungs to seize in his chest. What was she doing?

"Your shirt…" Her voice drifted off.

He felt her fingertips gently brush the puckered skin along his neck before straightening his shirt collar. The innocent touch sent a jolt of heat through his body. It was so simple, so unplanned, and yet it was the first time a woman had touched his scars.

His foster mother had often kissed and patted his cheek, and nurses had applied medicine and bandages after various reconstructive procedures, but this was different. As a shiver ran down his spine, it *felt* different, as well.

Without thinking, he brought his hand up to grasp hers. Sam gasped softly at his sudden movement, but she didn't pull away when his scarred fingers wrapped around her own. He was glad. He wasn't ready to let go. His every nerve lit up with awareness, and he was pretty certain she felt it, too. Her dark brown eyes were wide as she looked at him, her moist lips parted seductively and begging for his kiss.

He slowly drew her hand down, his eyes locked on hers. Sam swallowed hard and let her arm fall to her side when he finally let her go. "Much better," she said, gesturing to his collar with a nervous smile. She held up the flash drive in her other hand. "I'll get this printed for you, sir."

"Call me Brody," he said, finding his voice when the air finally moved in his lungs again. He might still be her boss, but suddenly he didn't want any formalities between them. He wanted her to say his name. He wanted to reach out and touch her again. But he wouldn't.

Don't miss
A BEAUTY UNCOVERED by Andrea Laurence,
part of the Secrets of Eden miniseries, available
October 2013 from Harlequin® Desire.

HDEXP0913

HARLEQUIN®

Desire

YULETIDE BABY SURPRISE

by *USA TODAY* bestselling author
Catherine Mann

The holiday spirit has professional rivals Miriama and
Rowan caring for an abandoned baby—together. But when
playing house starts to feel all too real, will they say yes to
becoming a family?

This Billionaires and Babies novel is also part of
Catherine Mann's series The Alpha Brotherhood.
Don't miss any of the excitement!

An Inconvenient Affair
All or Nothing
Playing for Keeps

All available now from Harlequin® Desire!

Powerful heroes…scandalous secrets…burning desires.